Linc

SPECIAL MESSAGE TO READERS

This book is published under the auspices of

THE ULVERSCROFT FOUNDATION

(registered charity No. 264873 UK)

Established in 1972 to provide funds for research, diagnosis and treatment of eye diseases. Examples of contributions made are: —

A Children's Assessment Unit at Moorfield's Hospital, London.

•

Twin operating theatres at the Western Ophthalmic Hospital, London.

•

A Chair of Ophthalmology at the Royal Australian College of Ophthalmologists.

•

The Ulverscroft Children's Eye Unit at the Great Ormond Street Hospital For Sick Children, London.

You can help further the work of the Foundation by making a donation or leaving a legacy. Every contribution, no matter how small, is received with gratitude. Please write for details to:

THE ULVERSCROFT FOUNDATION,
The Green, Bradgate Road, Anstey,
Leicester LE7 7FU, England.
Telephone: (0116) 236 4325

In Australia write to:

THE ULVERSCROFT FOUNDATION,
c/o The Royal Australian and New Zealand
College of Ophthalmologists,
94-98 Chalmers Street, Surry Hills,
N.S.W. 2010, Australia

SUNLIT SECRETS

Connie Ruddick is all alone in the world. When she arrives in the California town of Ocasa, she has the chance to take a job as the local schoolteacher, but this chance is based on a lie. Handsome cowboy Nate Truman has his own secrets, but can he forgive Connie's deceit? She plans to leave before she is found out, but escaping from Nate and the warm-hearted people of Ocasa proves to be nigh on impossible.

Books by Sally Quilford
in the Linford Romance Library:

THE SECRET OF HELENA'S BAY
BELLA'S VINEYARD
A COLLECTOR OF HEARTS
MY TRUE COMPANION
AN IMITATION OF LOVE

SALLY QUILFORD

SUNLIT SECRETS

Complete and Unabridged

LINFORD
Leicester

First published in Great Britain in 2011

First Linford Edition
published 2012

British Library CIP Data

Quilford, Sally.
Sunlit secrets. - - (Linford romance library)
1. Love stories.
2. Large type books.
I. Title II. Series
823.9′2–dc23

ISBN 978–1–4448–1218–3

Published by
F. A. Thorpe (Publishing)
Anstey, Leicestershire

Set by Words & Graphics Ltd.
Anstey, Leicestershire
Printed and bound in Great Britain by
T. J. International Ltd., Padstow, Cornwall

This book is printed on acid-free paper

1

California, 1895

Connie stepped down from the train, into the intense midday heat. She did not expect anyone to meet her, so it was no surprise that the station was empty, apart from a porter. She asked him to take care of her luggage until she knew the outcome of her meeting.

It did surprise her five minutes later when she reached the centre of the southern Californian town of Ocasa that it, too, was deserted. She had expected it to be as busy as the other towns in which she had stopped en route. She longed to stop somewhere for a cool drink, but felt uncomfortable walking into the saloon alone. There did not seem to be a more suitable hostelry in the vicinity.

The town's main buildings, like the jail and the sheriff's office, were white-wash stucco, in the Spanish style. Some attempts had been made to beautify the town, adding flower beds on the town square, and touching up some of the municipal buildings. But for the most part it looked like what it was; an old border town, a heartbeat away from modernisation, with colonial-style buildings badly in need of a lick of paint. A few had broken windows. Further out of town, nestling in the hillside, were some pretty white villas, also in the Spanish style. Beyond them, adorning the landscape, were orange groves shimmering in the afternoon sun.

An elderly man, sitting on a rocking chair outside a tumbledown trading post, noticed her and growled, 'You'll find them all up at the school house, Ma'am.'

It wouldn't have surprised Connie to learn that the man had sat down at the age of twenty and had never moved from the spot. His face and bare arms were the same mahogany hue as the rocker, suggesting he had become a part of it.

'Oh . . . ' she murmured in response.

'You'll be the new schoolmarm from England, I reckon. We was expecting you a month ago.'

Connie should have corrected him then, but she was too tired and thirsty. 'How did they know to be at the schoolroom today?' she asked.

The idea of a welcoming committee filled her with dread. The news she had to impart was bad enough, without the whole town hearing it.

'They're not waiting on you, Ma'am. They're discussing them bandits.'

He spoke as if Connie should automatically know what he was talking about. 'I'd go up myself, and have my say, but it'd take me all day to climb up there. Besides no one listens to an old-timer like me any more. Mined this area for gold, man and boy, I did, long before these European settlers came in. I knows all the hideouts and . . . '

'I'd better go and see them,' said Connie, who was almost wilting in the heat. She had no doubt his life was fascinating, but she would rather be out of the sun. Bidding him a polite farewell, she walked towards the white-washed schoolhouse, which was set on a hill above the town. All around it and behind it oranges grew, shining like golden orbs in the sun.

It was the prettiest sight that Connie had ever seen, and had she not been so weary from travel, she might have enjoyed it more. It was a pity she would not be able to spend more time exploring the landscape. She bolstered herself up, ready to pass on her message and then, after a night's rest, return home. To what, she did not know. That was a bridge she would cross when she came to it.

As the old man had said, the townsfolk were in the schoolhouse. The porch door had been left open to let in fresh air, such as there was. Connie stepped up onto the porch, but went no further. From her vantage point, she could see people sitting in rows, whilst others stood around, leaning on the walls, fanning themselves with pieces of paper which she guessed to be flyers announcing the meeting. Some of the flyers lay on the floor at her feet.

Babies whimpered in their mothers' arms, whilst older children sat cross-legged on the floor, occasionally swatted by a parent's hand when they talked too loudly. The old man at the trading post had not been exaggerating when he said the whole town was at the meeting.

'So it's about time we did something about Frank Hunter and his men,' a barrel-chested man in his fifties was saying. 'This land is supposed to be settled now, yet we're still getting bandits riding in and creating chaos in our peaceful town.'

The speaker's lower face was covered in a fine set of ginger whiskers that he clearly cultivated with pride. Above the beard and moustache, he had similar weather-beaten features to the old man in the rocking chair. In fact, the whole congregation had the look of people who spent many hours working in the sun — or, more likely, had Spanish ancestry, as Connie found out later. She felt pasty by comparison.

'We called in the US Marshalls, Joshua,' answered another man. He too was middle-aged, but clean-shaven and handsome with distinguished silver-grey hair. His English accent, with only a hint of the local drawl, immediately identified him to Connie as Reverend Christopher Youlgreave. He was the man she had travelled to see.

'They should be here in a week or two,' the churchman continued. 'Until then, I urge you all not to take the law into your own hands. We've avoided bloodshed so far . . .'

'Yes, by giving Hunter what he wants,' retorted Joshua. 'Reverend, I know you ain't one for sinning and you've got to warn us against all that, but we've got to protect our families, our cattle and our crops.'

'I'm glad you put your family first there, Joshua,' said someone in the crowd. 'Otherwise I'd be afraid you were only upset because one of your calves was stolen. You'd been quiet enough on this subject 'til then.'

'I needed that calf to feed my family,' growled Joshua. 'If you can afford to lose stock, Abraham, then you're a lucky man, but I can't. No one here can. Without these bandits, Ocasa could be a prosperous town. With them coming in every few weeks taking away the fruits of our labour, we're barely breaking even.'

'That's still no excuse for becoming vigilantes,' persisted Reverend Youlgreave. 'It can only end badly, and not necessarily for the bandits. There are women and children here. So far, Hunter has left them alone. If we start sending guns after him, he may turn. I've heard he was involved with a gang in Chicago who . . .'

'Yeah, yeah, we all know that story,' said Joshua, putting up his hand. 'Let me give you a list of what's been stolen this time. Not just from me. The Claytons lost some wheat from their stores. The Grants lost a couple of horses. Old Tom's trading post got broken into and some farming tools were stolen. A shovel, a rake, some rope and some canvas, plus some blasting caps. What they want those for, I ain't daring to guess. Then last night they ride into town, drunk as skunks, and smash windows.'

That explained the damage Connie had seen on her way to the schoolhouse.

'Some of us chased them off. It could have been much worse. We've been working hard to make this town a fine place for us all to live,' Joshua continued, 'but if Hunter is stocking up before he goes up into the hills for winter, chances are he'll be back before the US Marshalls reach us, and all our efforts will be wasted.'

'We should get Nate Truman to deal with him,' said a small boy of about ten, sitting on the floor. He was a beautiful child, with dark skin and black eyes. 'There's this man they write about in *Outlaws and Bandits* and it sounds just like him. A law-abiding man who turned cold-blooded killer. They say he's just like Jesse James. The way they describe him, with that scar on his cheek an' all, he sounds just like Mr Truman.'

'Now, Billy,' said Joshua, shaking his head. The fond look he gave the child suggested a family relationship belied by their different complexions. 'Truman don't have anything to do with folks in the town. He just stays up at that ranch of his.'

Connie noticed that no one, not even Joshua, refuted what Billy had said. In fact, she noticed some apt looks, particularly from the women, when Billy first mentioned Truman's name.

'It's him, Grandpa, I know it is.' The boy's eyes shone with eagerness.

'Billy . . . ' Joshua looked about to say something indulgent when his eyes alighted on something or someone near the back of the room.

'I'm sure we don't want to be accusing our neighbours of wrongdoing. Mr Truman is well-respected around here.'

'Would you have said that if you

hadn't realised I was sitting at the back of the room?' A deep, resonant voice spoke from amongst the crowd. There was a bustle of movement, and a tall, lean, dark man stepped into the aisle. He had his back to Connie, so she couldn't see his face, but she instinctively felt the power emanating from his broad shoulders. The muscles on his arms rippled through the sleeves of his clean white shirt. He wore black denims and a leather waistcoat, with camel-coloured chaps and black boots.

'I got no argument with you, Nate, you know that,' said Joshua immediately. 'We been good neighbours, as far as I know. But . . . well, since you're here, you must know what's been going on, even if you don't come into town much.'

'Yeah, I know. My ranch hand, Curly, told me there was a meeting. I wasn't invited, but I came anyway.'

'You don't normally accept our invitations,' said Reverend Youlgreave with a small smile.

'No, that's true enough,' agreed the man called Nate. 'I'm not much of a one for socialising. But I had no idea that such . . . legends . . . had grown up around me.'

'All I'm saying is,' said Joshua, who appeared to be choosing his words carefully, 'is that if you were that man — well, then, maybe you'd be able to help us.'

'Listen to the Reverend, Joshua,' said Nate. 'Wait for the Marshalls to arrive and sort this out. Otherwise innocent people could end up dead.'

'And meanwhile Hunter just keeps coming into town, rustling cattle and damaging our property. I'm guessing your property is safe.' Joshua's lips set in a thin line.

'I got guards on the gate to make sure of it. No one gets on or off my land without me knowing it.'

'Well we ain't got the men or the money to do that,' Abraham cut in.

'I'm happy to loan you some of my men for a few weeks as long as the sheriff is willing to deputise them so that they don't end up facing the hangman. Where is Sheriff Palmer, by the way? Shouldn't he be here?' Nate looked around the room and Connie was able to catch a tantalising glimpse of him. He had a strong profile, tanned, but not as weather-beaten as the other townspeople. A long, thin scar ran from his cheekbone to his mouth, and whilst it should have looked unattractive, it only added to his powerful aura.

'The sheriff is in jail,' said Joshua, rolling his eyes. 'He had a little too much to drink in the Sunset Saloon last night, so the deputy locked him up for his own good. We could do with a new sheriff.' Joshua looked hopefully towards Nate.

Nate shook his head. 'I'm not the man you want.' He turned to the group of children and his voice softened, tinged with amusement. 'No matter what young Billy here would have you believe about me. As for the scar on my face, Billy, let it be a lesson to you to choose your barber carefully.' Connie could not actually see it, but she had the distinct impression that Nate winked at the child.

'Aw,' said Billy, his shoulders slumping. 'I was so sure.'

For some reason, Connie felt the same disappointment as the child. She wanted Nate Truman to be a man she could trust, which was ridiculous since she did not even know him. If he was a cold-blooded killer, she should not even want to! Maybe it would be best to just turn around and go home, this very moment.

'We'll arrange with the sheriff to deputise your men,' said Joshua. 'Thank you, Nate. Maybe . . . well, me and Martha are having a barn raising on Sunday. Maybe you'd like to come.'

'Thank you, but no,' said Nate. He didn't apologise or make any excuses, which was how Connie was used to such things being done in the small English town in which she grew up.

'Well,' replied Joshua, 'the invitation

is open. You can come or you can stay away. It makes no difference to me, I'm sure.' He looked as if he was about to spit on the floor, then seemed to remember he was in mixed company, and instead swallowed hard.

'Thank you for coming down, Nate,' said Reverend Youlgreave. 'I think that I speak for us all when I say that your company is always most welcome here, in town and in the church.'

There was a quiet rebuke in Youlgreave's voice when he mentioned the church.

'I've told you before, Reverend, I'm not a religious man,' said Nate, quietly. Connie's eyes widened in shock. As the daughter of a vicar, the idea of not attending church was unthinkable.

Nate became more businesslike. 'I suggest we put some lookouts on the highest points of the town, on a shift basis. Four hours on, four hours off, so they don't get too tired and fall asleep. Like I said, I'll loan some of my men, but they can't do it all.'

'Don't worry, Nate,' answered Joshua.

'We're all willing to pull our weight.' Was there another rebuke in those words? Connie suspected there was — because whilst Nate offered men, he clearly insisted on keeping out of things himself.

'I'll do anything I can — inside the law — but I'm not willing to get involved in a lynching party.' Nate turned suddenly and strode from the schoolroom, almost knocking Connie over in the process.

'Sorry, Ma'am, I didn't see you there,' he said.

Their eyes met and Connie felt something pierce her heart. His eyes were flint-grey, but full of some unspoken emotion that she felt mirrored her own. For a brief moment in time that, conversely, seemed to last an eternity, they were kindred spirits, both having suffered the same loss.

She shook her head a little, to get rid of the fanciful thoughts, only to find they persisted.

'No, I'm sorry. I was in your way,' she murmured. Despite her words, Connie found she was quite unable to move.

'Who is that?' said Reverend Youlgreave. 'Do I detect an English accent?' He walked along the aisle and onto the porch. 'Is it Elizabeth Bradford? When you didn't arrive a month ago, we thought you'd decided not to come.'

He gave Connie a welcoming smile and held out his hand.

Connie should have corrected him then. It would be the right thing to do. But her decision was made rashly and once the lie was out, she could not turn back without seeming foolish.

'Reverend Youlgreave?' She held out her hand, disturbed to see that it trembled slightly. 'It's been a very long time, hasn't it? I apologise for my late arrival, but my younger sister . . . Constance . . . who was travelling with me, took ill on the journey.'

'And — where is she now?' asked the Reverend gently, as if he had already seen the answer in her eyes.

'I'm afraid she died. I would have written but . . . ' Connie's eyes filled with genuine tears, as she recalled her very real dilemma.

'No, no, I can well understand that your grief prevented it. Poor young Constance. She was — what? Only twenty? Such a sad loss, and I was looking forward to meeting her at last.' Reverend Youlgreave turned to Truman, who was still standing there, watching Connie with his handsome head tipped to one side and a thoughtful look on his face.

'Let me introduce you to Mrs Elizabeth Bradford. Her father, Charles Ruddick, and I studied theology together.'

'Mrs Bradford.' Nate tipped his hat. 'I'm happy to meet you. Please accept my condolences about your sister. Will your husband be joining you soon?'

'No, no, I am a widow,' said Connie, tripping over her words, with the sinking realisation that one lie had led to another and would probably lead to many more. 'My husband died eighteen months ago.'

'Then please accept my condolences

again. It must be hard for someone as young as you to have to start again.'

'She certainly looks very young,' said Reverend Youlgreave as if the thought had only just occurred to him. 'The last time I saw you was twenty years ago, when you were — what? Eight years old? You've hardly aged at all. It's that good English air. I hope you're sensible and keep out of the California sun.'

'Actually,' said Connie, remembering how tired and thirsty she was. 'I've travelled a long way in the heat and . . . '

'Oh, of course, you poor child. And here we are, keeping you talking. Come with me. I'll get my wife, Sofia, to fix you up some lemonade and something to eat. Mr Truman.' The Reverend tipped his hat.

'Reverend. Mrs Bradford . . . '

Connie stole a look back at him as Reverend Youlgreave led her back towards the town, and the whitewashed house at the side of the church. Nate knew the truth, she was convinced of it

— or at least suspected it.

Yet even if he did suspect, he could hardly call her a liar. There was no one left alive — at least, in America — who could say that she was not Elizabeth.

2

The journey from England had been an arduous one. But her sister, Elizabeth, had felt that both she and Connie needed a change of scenery. The death of not just Elizabeth's husband, George, but also their mother and father, had left them with just each other for company.

Unfortunately their circumstances had not left them with very much money. George had left Elizabeth one hundred pounds a year to live on, and Connie had an even smaller annuity from her parents, which would only come into force when she was twenty-one. It was not enough for both of them in a society which frowned upon women who worked.

That was when Elizabeth hit upon the bright idea of moving to America. 'Women are allowed to work over there,' she told Connie. 'Some even become doctors. Or journalists, or ranch owners. I heard of one girl from our town that went over to America and took over a vineyard. That was years ago so things will have moved on even further.'

'Are you thinking of growing grapes, Lizzie?' asked Connie.

'No, silly. Do you remember how father used to go on about Reverend Youlgreave? I met him once. He was a flamboyant character; very handsome and charming, as I remember.'

'Oh yes, the one who threw up his living here and went off to America. There was some scandal, wasn't there?'

'That's the one. Father was writing to him right up to the end. I thought I'd write to ask him if he could advise me of any positions I might take over there. You could come with me and we'll both be able to find work.'

Connie remembered looking around her, hating the idea of leaving their home. They might not have family left, but there were neighbours and friends who cared for them. But Elizabeth, who was eight years older and with an irrepressible enthusiasm for life, no matter what it threw at her, was always able to talk her around.

It seemed like a small miracle when Reverend Youlgreave replied and said that not only could he advise them of employment, but that the small town in which he lived was looking for a schoolmistress, due to the previous incumbent having just married.

'You could be a schoolmistress again here,' Connie had said to her at the time. It was what Elizabeth had done before she had met her husband George.

'Connie, dearest . . . ' Elizabeth had taken her by the hand. 'I know that I give the impression that I cope well with everything. But losing George so soon after Mother and Father . . . I need to get away from this place of death and loss. And I think you do, too. I certainly cannot leave without you.

You're all I have left. Please say you'll come with me.'

'Of course I'll come with you, darling.'

Elizabeth had taken ill in a small town halfway across America. If Connie ever knew the name of the town, she'd wiped it from her memory. What she could not forget was Elizabeth's sudden loss of vitality as a fever struck her during an overnight stop. Connie nursed her elder sister for three weeks, helped by the local doctor, who was drunk most of the time, but kindly waived his fee when he realised Connie's predicament. She suspected he hoped she would thank him in some other way, but he did not press that point when she made it clear she was not interested.

And then Elizabeth had died in her arms, leaving her alone and lost in a strange land.

It left Connie with a dilemma. They brought very little money with them. Enough for the trip, with Elizabeth making arrangements with the bank in England to forward money to their new home. Most of the money they had on them had been spent on the bedroom they rented in a rundown hotel during Elizabeth's illness.

Luckily Elizabeth had paid for all their tickets across America. Connie did not have enough money to return home, and would have nothing even if she could make it back to Britain, Elizabeth's annuity having died with her. But she could get to Ocasa.

She did not intend to lie. Her original plan was to throw herself at the mercy of Reverend Youlgreave and ask if she could simply take Elizabeth's place as the schoolmistress. She knew her age and lack of experience were against her, so had fully expected to be sent home on the next train.

On her first night in Ocasa, when she settled down to sleep in the first comfortable bed for many months, she told herself that she had no other choice than to lie. If she had told the truth, there was nothing to stop the Reverend telling her no, meaning she would have to return home.

Common sense, restored by a decent meal, plenty to drink and a restful afternoon sitting on the porch, told her that he would have done no such thing. He was a kind man, who would not let her be alone in the world once he knew her predicament.

But Connie had been so worn out by travel, grief and fear of the future that she hardly had time to think before she allowed the lie to take hold. There was no going back. The Reverend might well be kind, but he might not forgive deceit. Added to which, once the fib was out there, she felt too embarrassed to own up. She fell asleep believing she had no choice but to continue to live the lie.

* * *

'Did you sleep well?' asked Sofia, when Connie went down to breakfast the next morning. Sofia had been something of a surprise. Most vicars' wives in England were matronly types, and sometimes even more disapproving than their husbands. Sofia was a stunningly beautiful dark-eyed Spaniard, not much older than thirty, dressed in an off-the-shoulder blouse and loose-fitting patterned skirt. She was also heavily pregnant with her first child.

'Very well, thank you. Oh, do let me do that.'

Sofia was lifting up a heavy pan of bacon and eggs. 'No, no, you sit down. I keep telling Christopher that I am pregnant, not ill.'

'Yes, but you've taken care of me enough. That glass of lemonade was probably the best I've ever tasted.'

'You have had a long, tiring journey, I know. You need to regain your strength. You are going to need it. Especially for my little nephew, Billy.'

'Billy is your nephew?'

'Si. My brother, Paolo, he married Joshua's girl, Emma. You will find we are nearly all related in some way around here. We intermarry a lot. That is why I snapped up Christopher when he arrived here. So I would not have to marry one of my cousins!' Sofia laughed.

'How long have you been married?'

'Eight years now. It has taken this long for the Lord to bless us with a child.' She genuflected and kissed the crucifix she wore around her neck.

'You're a Catholic? Does that . . . I mean, is it a problem?'

'You mean being married to a Protestant minister? No. We are very liberal around here. Also, there are not so many men to go around, so beggars cannot be choosers.'

Again Sofia laughed. Connie imagined that the house must be filled with her musical laughter all day. No wonder Reverend Youlgreave had not wanted to return to England.

'I am sorry you missed the sunset last night,' her hostess went on.

'I'm sorry too. I was exhausted. I

know it's supposed to be wonderful. The Reverend said something about it being pink.'

'Si. It turns the sky pink. It is as pretty as a picture. Ocasa — the name of the town — it means sunset.'

'I didn't know that.'

'Yes, the Spaniards who first came here in the fifteen hundreds saw the sunset and knew that the town could not be called anything else.'

'I'll do my best to stay awake for it tonight. Now, I need to work out where I'm going to live.'

Sofia put a plate of bacon and eggs in front of Connie before waving her hand dismissively. 'You will live with us here. We have plenty of room. There is a cottage for the schoolmistress, but you do not want to live there alone. It is on the edge of town, and the bandits have used it to hide in since the last schoolmistress married. They have left it in a mess. Oh, you do not want to live there.'

'All the same, I would like to see it. I

can't impose on you for too long.'

'You are alone in the world, but we would not have you feel lonely, Elizabeth. It is right if I call you Elizabeth, is it not? I feel that we are friends already, and we are very informal here. Not like in England. Christopher had to leave that place.' Sofia rolled her eyes as if she personally hated England for not being good enough for her husband. 'And if you ask me, a married woman had no right to be setting her sights on a man of God.'

Connie tried to hide her surprise. She knew Christopher Youlgreave had to leave England under something of a cloud, but the details had been kept from her.

'But,' Sofia continued, as if she had not just revealed a shocking secret about her husband, 'I always tell him that his personality is too big for any land, even one as big as America.' She laughed again. 'So I may call you, Elizabeth, si?'

'Er . . . Lizzie. Most people call me

Lizzie.' Connie looked down at her food, sinking deeper into her deceit, and hoping that Sofia would not notice her blushes. She also hoped fervently that she would remember to answer when anyone addressed her as Lizzie — or as Mrs Bradford.

Sofia poured them both a cup of coffee, and sat down at the table whilst Connie ate. 'Your late husband — George, was he not? What did he do?'

'George was a school inspector . . . they . . . we met when he came to inspect the school at which I taught.'

'He was handsome, yes?'

'Not especially, no. But he was kind and thoughtful, and . . . ' She almost said 'Lizzie', but managed to check herself. ' . . . I'd been jilted by a previous beau, just a week before our wedding. So when dear, good George came along, proving that men could be kind and reliable, I thought I should snap him up.'

'You were jilted? But you are so pretty, with that red hair and those big green eyes. The man was a fool, but it was lucky for George.'

'I was lucky, too. He was always so good with me and my sister.'

'Constance? Yes, Christopher told me about her. It is so sad that she is not with us.' Sofia genuflected and kissed her cross again. 'Was she very pretty like you?'

'Oh, my sister was much lovelier,' said Connie, thinking of Elizabeth, then reddened when she remembered she was actually supposed to be talking about herself. 'Everyone thought so . . . ' Her voice trailed away.

'It is painful to talk about, si? I understand. You and George, you were not blessed with children?'

'No. We always hoped, but . . . '

'Si, but now you are here you will find a new husband.'

'With a shortage of men?' Connie smiled, showing pretty dimples. She was on safer ground, talking about the present rather than the past.

'I think those who have been hiding

will suddenly appear now there is a new woman in town,' said Sofia. 'Maybe even Nate Truman. Christopher said he seemed to be taking an interest in you yesterday.'

'Was he?' Connie suspected that Nate had other reasons for being interested — because he did not believe her story. Or perhaps that was simply her own guilt gnawing at her. 'Tell me about him.'

'Ah, si, he is handsome, is he not?' Sofia smiled knowingly. 'And perhaps not as reliable as your husband, George, and that is attractive to a woman sometimes. A man with a past.' Sofia sighed, theatrically fanning her hand in front of her face. 'He makes the heat rise, si? No one really knows him. He turned up here about five years ago, and moved into the ranch up on the cliff. You know that the sea is only three miles from here?'

'No, I didn't know. I've rather lost track of where I am.'

'Si, it is true. We must take you there

one day. The view over the Pacific Ocean, when the sun sets, is divine. Anyway, Nate Truman showed up here five years ago, and I think I can count on the fingers of one hand how many times he has come into the town. Mostly he sends his men here to do business for him. He does not socialise, and whilst he seems to be a good man, many legends have grown up around him.'

'Yes — your nephew, Billy, had him down as a cold-blooded killer.'

'Si, we live in a place where everyone knows everyone else's business, so for someone to keep their past from us . . . It is strange. That is when legends grow. If there are gaps, we fill them in ourselves. It is human nature in a place where nothing much happens.'

Sofia paused and smiled. 'Me, I think it was a woman. A man like that, there will have been many women, I am sure. Whoever she was, she broke his heart and he has come here to hide from the world. His ranch is called Melissa. I think she is behind all this.'

'I wonder how he really got the scar,' said Connie, resting her chin on her hand and completely giving herself up to Sofia's fantasy about Nate. 'He said it was down to a bad barber, but . . . '

'I know, it is more exciting to think he got it in a fight, si?'

Connie laughed. 'Perhaps he did. Perhaps his real story is that he was a bandit once upon a time but saw the error of his ways and now wants to live a good, clean life.'

'Oh, si, that is romantic. I like that idea. Perhaps the woman he was in love with died, and that is what made him turn good.'

They carried on in that vein for a while, each trying to outdo the other in a romantic back story for Nate Truman, whilst bonding as women.

It felt good for Connie to laugh, after so many weeks of grief and pain. She was even able to put aside the fact that she was living a lie, if only for a short time. By the time she helped Sofia clear away the breakfast dishes, they were firm friends.

3

'Come,' said Sofia, when the last of the plates were stacked away. 'I will show you the town, and we will take the buggy up into the hills.'

'I don't want to impose on you, Sofia. Are you sure you shouldn't be resting?'

'Has Christopher been talking to you? I will tell you what I tell him. I am pregnant, not ill. Besides, I go mad in this house. I have read every book we own, and we are waiting for new volumes to arrive from up the coast. We are sadly not so civilised that we have our own printing press nearby. So every week I wait for the train to bring more. Only some weeks they do not arrive. But that is good this week, as the train brought you instead — and you are much more interesting.'

'I have some books in my luggage.

Charles Dickens, Charlotte Brontë, and others. If you haven't already read them.'

'Then I will look through them later, but for today you must see our beautiful Ocasa. If you are not too tired, that is.'

'I feel much better today and I'd love to see the town.'

* * *

'You love it here, don't you?' said Connie, some time later as she and Sofia stood in a pretty orange grove above the town. They could see the town spread out below them. Men were working on repairing the damage to windows, and from her vantage point, Connie could see that there was much more of Ocasa than she first thought. It was a town where everyone had plenty of space in which to move. Charming whitewashed villas rested on the hillside amongst the orange groves, and even in the town, apart from the busy main street, houses had large front gardens and back yards in which grew orange, lemon and lime trees. As well as the cultivated groves, it seemed that everyone had their own individual supply of fresh fruit. Sofia had told her that citrus fruits had been introduced to the area by the Spaniards in medieval times, and the sale of the fruit contributed much to the town's finances.

Connie's old home in England had been in the countryside, but everything in the village had been huddled close together, with higgledy piggledy houses nestled in close rows. It had been comforting, especially in winter, when houses seemed to share whatever warmth there was. There was no need of that in Ocasa, with year-round sunshine. The town had a warmth of its own, which showed in the townspeople's welcoming smiles once they realised Connie was the new schoolmistress.

To the east she could just make out a stretch of blue sea, amongst the undulating hills. To the west stretched a snow-topped mountain range.

'They are the mountains where Hunter hides out,' Sofia explained. 'You must never go there alone. It is dangerous.'

'It's amazing that in this day and age such men still exist,' remarked Connie, shaking her head.

'You must remember that we are only twenty years away from this being a border town and frontier post,' Sofia explained. 'Only recently towns like Ocasa were considered beyond the civilised borders of America, at least by the white man. They did not think that we Mexicans might have our own moral codes. They thought Ocasa was only fit for stopping off on a journey to somewhere else. Usually outlaws, heading across the border into Mexico.

'We — my family and I — lived among the hills, and only came into town if we needed supplies because it was so dangerous. The gunslingers who came here, and some of the Europeans who were said to be civilised, treated us like the outsiders. When I was a little girl, a white man spat at me in the street and I could not understand why. Was I not the same as he?' She shrugged and smiled. 'In a very short time, and with Christopher's help, we have learned to live together and tame this town. Now my brother is married to Joshua's daughter, and I am married to Christopher, and no one cares. The townspeople are just happy for us.

'But the gunslingers and troublemakers who are no longer welcome here have gone even further onto the wrong side of the law, simply stealing what they want — and all because they do not know how to fit into this new, civilised West.'

'You sound as if you feel sorry for them.'

'I too have been the outcast, living in the hills. Si, I am sorry for them. If they cannot learn to live in this new world and treat it with respect as we all do, then their only option is to die in it. That is sad.'

'Yes. Yes, you're right — it is very

sad,' Connie agreed thoughtfully.

'It is getting late and I must prepare food for Christopher. We will eat, then later go and look at the sea.'

Connie was feeling rather tired, but did not like to say so. They climbed onto the buggy and rode back to the town.

'You are warm, si?' Sofia glanced across at her.

'Yes, I'm not used to such heat.'

'After lunch comes the siesta. It is the Spanish way.'

Connie was relieved to hear that.

'Also,' Sofia continued, 'we will find you different clothes. These thick dresses you wear are not good in this heat.'

This worried Connie a little. She could not see herself dressed in a sultry off-the-shoulder blouse like the one Sofia wore.

'I'm not sure . . . ' she stammered.

'No, no, not like this. Your poor pale skin would burn to a crisp. But we can find thinner material for you to wear. I am good at making clothes. I make them for all the European ladies.'

'There's no need to go to so much trouble, Sofia, my sister had some summer dresses. I brought them with me, since she wouldn't be using them. But she was a bit taller than me so I need to take them up. I haven't had the chance whilst travelling.'

Common sense had told her it would be foolish to leave the clothes behind in the town where Lizzie died. She did not have enough money to think of wasting good fabric. But ever since then, distaste at wearing her dead sister's clothes had overtaken her good sense. Connie could barely bring herself to look at Lizzie's belongings, let alone wear them, for fear of grief overwhelming her.

'Good — I will help you. Before we go home, we will call at the store for yarn and needles, si? I do not think you will have that in your suitcase.'

'Only a small sewing kit.'

When they reached the trading post, Old Tom sat on his rocker, where Connie had left him the day before. It surprised her when he actually got up and followed them inside.

'We are looking for yarn, Tomas. For Mrs Bradford. What colour, Lizzie?' Sofia inquired.

Connie had been so transfixed in looking at the array of articles Tom sold, from garden and farming implements to sacks of grain and more personal things that only ladies needed, she did not realise that Sofia was talking to her. The store was packed from floor to ceiling, leaving only a small space from the door to the counter for customers to stand.

'I'm sorry, Sofia,' she said. 'I've never seen so many different things in one place. It's like Aladdin's cave in here. White yarn will do, thank you.' Connie reached into her purse for some coins, panicking at the thought she might not have enough.

'No, no,' said Sofia. 'I too need yarn, and will probably use more.'

Connie blessed her for understanding. 'I'll pay you back when I can.'

'Ah, that reminds me, Mrs Bradford,' said Old Tom. 'The bank manager, Mr Fletcher, has been a-looking for you. Says he has business to discuss. He didn't say what, though I asked him. It's confidential, like.'

'Oh, thank you, Tom. I'd best go and see him. Do you mind, Sofia?'

'No. You go on. I will see you back at the house, si?'

As she was leaving, she heard Sofia remonstrating with Old Tom. 'You should not ask the bank manager what he wants with Mrs Bradford. Such things are private.' There was a miniscule pause before Sofia lowered her voice and said, 'Are you sure that Mr Fletcher did not say what it was?'

That made Connie smile rather than feel angry. Ocasa was clearly a town where secrets were considered bad. No wonder they were so intrigued by Nate Truman. Almost as if thinking of him conjured him up, she walked straight into him as she stepped off the trading post porch.

'Oh! I'm sorry, Mr Truman.'

'Morning, ma'am. How are you settling in?' He raised his hat.

'A little overwhelmed with everything at the moment. I'm just on my way to the bank.'

'Yes, I heard Mr Fletcher was looking for you.'

'News travels fast around here.'

'Oh, yeah. You are in the town with no secrets.'

'You manage quite well.' It was out before Connie realised that it sounded rude.

'Maybe it's because I don't have any.'

As she looked at his handsome face, she knew that was not true. He was too guarded — almost as if afraid his secret might slip out at any moment. She understood it, because she felt that way herself. The sense of them being kindred spirits filled her fantasies again.

'Do you like Ocasa?' he asked, when she did not respond to his previous statement.

'Yes, it's very pretty. And I'm sad to

hear that the bandits are causing so much trouble.'

'Do I detect a note of reproach there?'

'What? Oh no, of course not, Mr Truman. You're quite right in that such things should be left to the authorities.'

But was she not a little disappointed that he was not a knight in shining armour? She dismissed the thought. He did not have to be anyone's hero, least of all hers.

'I really ought to go and see Mr Fletcher. It's nice to see you again.'

'You too, Mrs Bradford. I hope I'll be seeing more of you.'

As she walked away, Connie wondered if he really meant it — or whether he was just being polite.

* * *

Mr Fletcher was a bald-headed man, who looked somewhat harassed by his duties, despite the fact that his clientele could not have numbered more than one hundred local farmers and ranchers.

'Mrs Bradford. It's nice to meet you, finally. I was at the meeting yesterday, when you arrived, but of course no one got the chance to speak to you before the Reverend whisked you away. As well he should, after your long journey. May I join everyone in adding my condolences for the loss of your young sister, Constance? And of course of your husband, Mr George Bradford. Please, sit down.'

Nate Truman had been right about no one having any secrets in Ocasa. Connie sat down in the cluttered office. If she wanted, she could have opened any file from the desk and found out the financial affairs of anyone in the town. Nothing appeared to be locked away. She wondered how many people did just that when Mr Fletcher left the office.

'Thank you,' she said. 'What did you wish to see me about?'

'Why, your annuity, of course. You

arranged to have it transferred to our bank on a monthly basis.'

'Oh yes, I'd forgotten,' said Connie, feeling more panicked than ever. It was not her annuity. It was Lizzie's. She had completely forgotten about it, and only had some vague idea that if anything happened to Lizzie it would revert to one of George Bradford's cousins. But, of course, it could not do that if she did not inform the relevant authorities of her sister's death.

'I wondered how you wanted it paid. Did you want the cash every month, or just a small amount on which to live weekly? With local taxes and exchange rates it won't be worth as much as in England, but you can live quite comfortably here on what's left. There's not much to buy but yarn in Old Tom's, despite his shelves being full.'

Connie's eyes widened. That news had spread fast! She tried to recall if anyone else was in the store, and remembered an elderly woman walking out as they were walking in, and a child playing on the porch. She blushed, remembering that she had let Sofia pay. Did everyone know that, too?

'And of course, you'll receive your salary when you start teaching.'

'I, erm . . . I think I'll leave it in the bank,' said Connie, thinking rapidly about how to sort things out. She would have to write to England and tell them what happened to Lizzie. To take the money would be fraud.

But if she told the bank in England about Lizzie, then Mr Fletcher would find out — and then she had no doubt that the whole town would know as quickly as they found out she was buying yarn. The easiest thing to do would be to tell the truth now, but her sense of shame stopped her.

'May I say that's very sensible of you? Now I just need your signature on some documents, so that . . . '

'My signature?'

'Yes, of course, to complete the transfer of funds. I know you signed in England, but we have our own laws.'

'Oh yes, I understand. Silly me. I wonder . . . actually, Mr Fletcher, I'm not feeling very well.' Connie put her hand to her head, not really having to feign illness. She felt sick with worry. 'I'm not used to this heat and I'm still very tired from my long journey. Could I do this another day when my head is a little clearer? My father always told me I should read legal documents carefully and I'm in no fit state to concentrate at the moment.'

It was a good excuse and not exactly a lie. Her father had taught both his daughters that they should always read the small print.

'Your father was a very wise man, Mrs Bradford. I apologise for bothering you. It was just that I thought you might need funds . . . '

Connie was beginning to understand why Nate Truman played his cards so close to his chest. It was impossible to have a private life in Ocasa. Yet there was nothing insidiously nosy about the inhabitants — unlike an old lady who had lived near to Connie and Lizzie in England and who spread gossip in a nasty way that destroyed reputations. It seemed to Connie that in Ocasa, everyone learned each other's secrets as a way of taking care of people. You were short of money; someone else bought you yarn. You arrived with nothing but your baggage, the bank manager was on hand to make sure you received what you were entitled to. She wondered why the bandits felt the need to come and rob the town. All they had to do was turn up hungry and tired, and within five minutes someone, most probably Sofia, would make sure they were fed and had a warm bed to sleep in.

'Yes, that's very thoughtful of you,' she said to Mr Fletcher. 'Thank you for your kindness and understanding.'

'If you do need money, I'd be more than happy to advance you some. No need to sign anything. I trust you, Mrs Bradford.'

Connie wanted to cry then. She blessed his kindness, but also suspected that if he did that, the whole town would know about it. They would probably find out that she had not signed the document either, but there was not much she could do about that. She needed to get away, to have time to work out how she could extricate herself from the ridiculous situation in which she had put herself.

She stood up, and muttered her thanks, then walked unsteadily from the office. As with the illness, she did not have to pretend. Her legs trembled beneath her.

She stepped out of the office into the sunlight, and straight into Nate Truman's arms, sinking against him as nausea overtook her.

'Hey, what's wrong?' His calm voice was as comforting and certain as his arms. Almost as if women fell into his arms every day. Not that she would be surprised to learn that they did.

'I'm afraid Mrs Bradford has taken unwell,' said Mr Fletcher. Connie did not even realise the bank manager followed her out. 'I was just about to help her back to the Youlgreaves' hacienda.'

'I'll take her,' said Nate. 'It'll give the town something else to talk about.' He led Connie from the bank and to a small buggy pulled by one horse. 'You can't walk in this heat. Get into the buggy.'

'Oh, it's not far and I don't want to be any more trouble than I have been already,' protested Connie, afraid that she might burst into tears at any moment.

He ignored her and put his hands around her slender waist, lifting her up onto the seat in one effortless movement.

He lifted her down just as easily when they reached the Youlgreave's home, and carried her up to the porch in his arms.

'I can walk,' she said. He ignored her.

'What is it?' said Sofia, rushing out of the house. 'Is Lizzie unwell?'

Nate briefly explained what had

happened, and was ushered into Connie's bedroom by Sofia. He set her down on the bed. When she tried to get up, Sofia pushed her back down.

'It is the heat,' said Sofia. 'Lizzie is not used to it. I told her, these clothes are no good in Ocasa. I was about to take up the hem on her summer dresses. But even in summer, these English wear such thick clothes, si?'

Connie looked around to see her bedroom in disarray. The trunk she had left packed the night before had been emptied. Clothes and books littered the top of the dresser, and were strewn over an armchair next to the window. It occurred to her that Sofia might have asked before going through her things, but she was too distraught to argue about it and also feared it would seem ungrateful. With relief she remembered there was nothing in her luggage to give away her secret. There was a photograph of her with Lizzie, but it did not indicate which sister was which. She had put the only picture of Lizzie and

George Bradford in Lizzie's grave.

Sofia left the room, to fetch Connie a drink.

'How are you feeling?' asked Nate.

'Better, thank you. I really don't need to be in bed.' Connie sat up and turned to sit on the edge of the mattress.

'You should stay here, where it's cool, for a while. If you're not used to this heat it can be hard going.' He was walking around the bedroom, picking up books and looking at the titles. '*Great Expectations*? It was one of my favourites when I was in college.' He flicked through the Charles Dickens novel, silently reading a few lines from one of the pages.

'Mine too. My father bought me that for Christmas just before he died.'

'Really?' He gave her a long look, then closed the book and put it back on the dresser.

'You went to college?'

'Yeah, but that was supposed to be a secret.' He smiled, showing even white teeth.

'Don't worry.' She smiled back. 'I'm not on the grapevine here yet.'

'Oh, you soon will be.' He folded his arms and leant back against the dresser. 'What are we going to do about you, hey?'

'What do you mean? Oh. Me fainting. Don't worry, Mr Truman. I'll keep out of the sun in future. I promise I don't make a habit of fainting in men's arms. I hate all that swooning stuff that some young girls do.'

'I should think so, you being a sensible, twenty-eight-year-old widowed lady.' Something in the way he said it made her look up sharply.

Sofia bustled back into the room, carrying a glass of lemonade. 'Now you must drink this, then rest, Lizzie. It is so good that you were outside the bank, Mr Truman. I do not know what Mr Fletcher was thinking, wanting her to read and sign legal documents on a hot day such as this when she has only just arrived.'

Connie did not bother asking how

Sofia knew what Mr Fletcher wanted her to do. The rapid spread of private conversations in Ocasa was a mystery that she guessed she would never fathom.

'I was waiting for Mrs Bradford, as a matter of fact,' said Nate. 'The sunset is even prettier from my porch, and I thought she'd enjoy seeing it. So I wanted to invite her . . . all of you . . . up to have dinner at my ranch tomorrow night.'

'Really?' Sofia looked astonished. 'We would be delighted, would we not, Lizzie? My goodness, when I tell Christopher he will be so excited. I do not mean to be rude, Mr Truman, but you do not normally invite people to your place.'

'Something I hope to amend.' Nate smiled. 'So the answer is yes?'

'Si, of course, si. Oh, Lizzie, is this not exciting? Now where is that pretty yellow dress I found? It is just right for tomorrow night.'

No one had actually asked Connie if

she wanted to go. The plans were made and decided upon without her.

As she watched a delighted Sofia bustle about, she decided she would probably never see Nate's house, as much as she would have liked to. She had to leave Ocasa — before everyone found out the truth about her.

But if Connie thought her arduous trip to the town had been beset by difficulties, she was soon to learn that leaving it would prove nigh on impossible.

4

'You missed another sunset, querida,' said Sofia reproachfully when Connie went to the kitchen the next morning.

'I'm sorry.' Her reply was tinged with guilt. Querida, she had quickly learned, was the Spanish word for darling. 'I think I'm still recovering from the travel.'

She had not exactly missed the sunset. She had been wide awake, and trying to work out how to get back home to England. Whilst lying there, absorbed in her problems, she had been vaguely aware of the light outside turning rose-coloured.

'You do not have to apologise, querida. I should not have made you do so much yesterday. It is my fault.'

'Sofia, you've been wonderful to me, really you have. I couldn't have asked for a better friend in my new home.'

Connie's voice broke on the last words.

'Perhaps you should go back to bed and rest for today. We have dinner tonight, and you want to look your best. Nate Truman's invitations are not just rare. They never happen. It is strange, the way he came down into the town two days in a row. As I told you yesterday, normally we do not see him at all. He sends his men. Christopher wondered what could have brought him — but he is a man, so he does not see the things that I see. Only one thing . . . one *person* . . . brought Mr Truman to town yesterday.' Sofia smiled knowingly, but Connie was at a loss to understand her.

'I don't want to go back to bed,' said Connie. 'Actually, I need to go and see Mr Fletcher.'

During the night, Connie had come to the decision that she would accept Mr Fletcher's offer of money up front, without having to sign anything. She reasoned that some of the money would have been paid in when Elizabeth was alive, whilst they were travelling, and she knew that her sister would not want to leave her without money, and would have gladly given Connie her last penny if she had known what would happen. So it would not *really* be stealing, or fraud. At least, that was how Connie justified it to herself, ignoring the niggling feeling that it was still the wrong thing to do. Then, she decided, she would go straight to the station and get the next train out. It would mean leaving behind most of her belongings, as it would be impossible to get them away without anyone noticing. But when she had dressed that morning, she'd put several extra layers on, so that she would at least have a change of clothes. She was already feeling the intense heat.

'No, no, no, no, no, querida,' said Sofia. 'There is no need. Nate Truman spoke to Mr Fletcher yesterday and the bank manager has agreed that signing the documents can wait for a while.'

'When did he do that?'

'Yesterday afternoon, whilst you were

resting. He came back and told us. He also suggested that Christopher give you an advance on your salary, to . . . what was the phrase he used? Si, *to tide you over,* he said. So it is here.' Sofia reached up to the dresser and brought down a small leather pouch, handing it to Connie. 'A month's salary in advance.'

'Oh . . . ' Connie slumped down in a chair at the big, round table. Her mind worked overtime. She could still just go to the station, and give Sofia some other excuse for going out. But that would most certainly be taking money under false pretences — and whatever else she did that might be wrong, she could not do such a thing to the Youlgreaves, who had treated her with nothing but kindness. She turned the pouch over in her hand. 'Sofia, I can't take this when I haven't earned it.'

'But you will, querida, you will. You are a good girl. We all know that.' There was something in her tone that made Connie look at her sharply, but Sofia had already turned back to the stove.

'We are having pancakes this morning. With syrup. Yesterday I thought you needed feeding up, you are so slender, but you seem to have filled out already this morning. I hope that was my bacon and eggs.' Sofia's musical laughter filled the kitchen. 'Later, if you are really sure you would like to go out, I will take you up to the mission.'

'The mission?'

'Si, it is the orphanage where most of the children you will teach live. I thought you would like to meet them.'

'Yes, I'd like that. I . . . er . . . I'll go and put this money away safely before breakfast,' said Connie, feeling hotter than ever under her layers of clothes.

'Change your clothes, querida,' Sophia said. 'You are wearing far too much. Put on the dress that I altered yesterday.'

The dress, one of Elizabeth's, was made of white muslin, with blue forget-me-nots sewn on to the bodice. It made Connie appear very young and spring-like, which was not exactly the way she wanted to look. She wanted to look older and more capable.

When she went back into the kitchen, Sofia clapped her hands together. 'You are so pretty. I have a silk shawl that you can wear over it, to stop the sun from burning your arms.'

After breakfast, wearing a duck egg blue silk shawl across her shoulders and bare arms, Connie set off with Sofia to the orphanage.

It was next to the sea, with its own beach, where the children played and collected seashells. Connie could not help but smile when she heard the happy laughter of the children, and saw the nuns rushing around trying to contain the more active orphans.

When she was younger, she had visited some English orphanages with her father, and both had been dismayed by how grim they were. The children were raised on ideas of hell and damnation, with the so-called Christian governors firmly blaming the inmates for their lot in life. Her father had tried hard to change things from the top, but found he was swimming against the tide. The governors were too comfortable on the donations they received, very little of which actually went to the care of the children.

The orphanage near the sea that Connie visited that morning was nothing like those places, despite being run by nuns. The children were happy and clearly well-fed, and the nuns good-natured and forgiving of all their little transgressions.

'I don't believe that the children are to blame for their circumstances,' said Sister Alice, the nun in charge of the mission, with emphasis as she showed Connie and Sofia around. She was Hispanic, but spoke perfect English. Her face was serenely beautiful, and its vitality made it difficult for Connie to guess her age. She might have been anywhere between fifty and seventy. 'I refuse to punish them for the sins of their parents. Most of whom died in dire circumstances, because their farms failed, or because hunger led them to a life of crime. We try to give the children a happy life, in the hopes that when they grow up and leave us, they will carry that happiness on to their new lives.' She smiled benignly. 'If you convince a child that they are born in sin, then there is no reason for them to avoid sin. They simply grow up believing they are prone to it. I hope you agree, Mrs Bradford; we're eager that the new schoolmistress understand and carry on our teaching. Unlike the last one.'

Sofia and the nun exchanged knowing nods.

'I agree completely,' said Connie, eager to know what had happened to the other schoolmistress, but too shy to ask. 'You speak very much as my father did. I know I'm going to love teaching them. Do I come here, or do they come to the school?'

'They will come to you. It is important, I think, that they are allowed to be amongst other children, so that they do not feel apart from this world. I trust, having met you, that you will not treat them any differently to the children who have families.'

'No, not at all,' said Connie. Her only problem would be not to favour the children, because of their circumstances, but she did not say that to Sister Alice. She suspected by the twinkle in Sister Alice's eye that she knew exactly what Connie was thinking.

'That is good. Let me show you the rest of the orphanage.'

The building was clean and bright, and the children slept in comfortable dormitories. 'They all have to help with cleaning,' said Sister Alice. 'I believe that children should do chores. But we do not treat them as our slaves, as I have heard some orphanages do. We were approached once by a manufacturer from the north who wanted the children to make rope. He offered us much money, but I said no. I will not have six-year-olds damaging their hands and eyesight on such work.'

'I've seen that,' answered Connie, sadly. 'In an orphanage my father and I visited in England.' She looked around the bright and cheerful dormitory. 'Do you ever find families for the children?'

'Some, but most people want babies or workhorses. We seldom have babies here, and as I have already indicated, my children are not slaves. When they are twelve years old, we find employers for them amongst the kind people of Ocasa, but by then we expect the children to be able to read and write, so that one day they may make their own choice. One of our boys won a scholarship to a very good school and became a lawyer.'

'That's wonderful!' exclaimed Connie. 'Can I meet the children now?'

'Of course. You are staying for lunch, are you not?' Sister Alice looked to Sofia for confirmation.

Sofia smiled in a secretive manner and responded, 'Si, Sister Alice. We are staying.'

Lunch was a simple meal of vegetable soup and bread, but there was plenty and no child was denied a second portion if they asked for it. Connie did not think she would ever remember the names of all the children, or work out who was who. There were several Bernardos, even more Marias, and four brothers named after the Gospel writers.

'When I am older,' said Matthew — or it might have been Mark, Luke or John — 'I am gonna be rich and take care of my brothers. And I'll buy Sister Alice a mansion to live in.'

'I do not want a mansion,' said Sister Alice, with a smile. 'But you can donate to the orphanage. When you are a rich man.'

'Oh, you can all come and live with me,' the boy said, earnestly.

'The only way people like us get rich,' said one of the Bernardos, a boy of about ten with a hangdog expression which made him look many years older than he was, 'is to rob a bank.'

'You don't really believe that, do you, Bernardo?' asked Connie.

'It is how my papa was going to get rich. But he died before he could.'

Connie exchanged glances with Sister Alice, who nodded as if to confirm Connie's suspicions.

'I'm sure that your papa wouldn't want you to do that,' said Connie gently and choosing her words carefully. 'Because it's very dangerous, and he would prefer you to be safe and happy.'

'I guess so,' said Bernardo. 'Some people say papa was a bad man for what he did. Do you think he was a bad man, Senora?'

'No, I think he was a desperate man,' said Connie. 'Because he loved you and wanted to put food on the table. But if you do your lessons well and learn to read and write, you can easily find a job so you won't have to do what he did. He'll be very proud of you, I know.'

'I already read and write very well. And in English.'

'That's wonderful. You'll be able to

help me with the smaller children.'

Bernardo's hangdog expression changed to one of delight. 'Then I could be a teacher when I am grown up.'

'I think that's a wonderful thing to want to do,' said Connie. 'Then you can help other children like yourself.'

'Si,' said Bernardo. 'I think that instead of robbing banks, I'll teach. It is much safer.'

Connie noticed Sister Alice and Sofia exchange another glance followed by a smile. They'd been doing that a lot during her visit to the orphanage. She hoped it meant she had said and done the right thing.

* * *

'Do you think Sister Alice likes me?' Connie asked Sofia when they were on the way home.

'Oh, si, querida. She likes you very much.'

'It's just that my sister was so much better at this sort of thing than me,' said

Connie, caught slightly off guard by the enjoyable morning at the orphanage. 'She instinctively knew the right thing to say to people, whereas I . . . I feel I get it wrong sometimes.'

'I think that your sister would have been very proud of the way you dealt with Bernardo,' said Sofia. 'He is a good boy, but he worships his dead father, seeing him as a desperado. Which he was in a way, but that does not mean Bernardo must take the same path.'

'It makes you think about the bandits, doesn't it?' said Connie. 'What sort of lives they've had that led them to live the way they do. No one is born bad, I am convinced of that.'

'I am not so sure, querida. Some people are, I think. I have known boys raised by loving parents who still grew up to do terrible things. There is something missing from them, I believe. Some sense of shame or conscience. Most of us grow up to know right from wrong, even if our parents or our God do not guide us. Society, with its laws, teaches us that it is wrong to kill or steal or to tell lies. But some . . . they do it anyway. They do not care who they hurt.'

Connie gazed off into the distance, feeling her own sense of shame burning within her. What might Sofia say of her if she knew she had lied? And how dare she teach the children who attend her school right from wrong, when she was committing such a dreadful wrong herself? Once more she felt the urge to run away, partly to avoid the shame if her lie was discovered, and partly because she felt she owed those who had shown her kindness more than to continue to lie to them.

'I'll need some supplies. Books, chalk and slates,' Connie said after a long pause. 'Where would I go to get them?'

'The school has all you need, querida.'

'Could we go there now, so I can check? Just in case?' Her idea was to pretend that there was some item she absolutely had to have, and then travel out of town to get it. Then she just would not return. She had no idea where she would go, but it would be somewhere that she didn't have to lie any more about who she really was.

Sofia did not need asking twice. She drove the buggy to the schoolroom where the townspeople had met just a couple of days before. It looked different now that it was empty. A little bit shoddy and dusty. It needed to be filled with children and the sound of their singing to bring it to life. Connie could imagine it, and despite her intention to leave, was already planning a lesson which she hoped would teach the children but also make them laugh.

'It is in need of repainting,' Sofia explained on seeing Connie's dismayed expression. 'Christopher has asked some of the men to come in at the weekend and prepare it for your start on Monday. He has also ordered new desks and chairs for the children. As you can see, the others are falling apart.

He said that until they arrive, the children will have to sit cross-legged on the floor. Is that acceptable?'

'Oh yes, of course.' Connie smiled. 'Where is the teaching equipment?' There was only an easel, holding a double-sided blackboard up on the small platform, near to the teacher's desk.

'In a closet, behind the blackboard.'

Though Connie had never taught, she had learned enough from Elizabeth to know that the school did indeed have everything it needed, including reading books and text books featuring maths and foundation science subjects.

'I think I would like to check that these textbooks are completely up to date,' said Connie. 'Where do you purchase them from?'

Sofia named a city to the north. Connie vaguely remembered passing through it on her way to Ocasa.

'I shall go there tomorrow and see for myself,' Connie said. 'I may even find better ones.'

'I will take you, querida.'

'No!' Connie spoke more firmly than she had intended. She softened her exclamation with a smile. 'Tomorrow you must rest. You have given up enough of your time to me. Besides, I would rather like to learn how to get around on my own. Not that I'm ungrateful for all you've done, don't think that for a minute.' Connie reached out and touched Sofia's arm.

She didn't know if she imagined it, but it seemed that Sofia's eyes narrowed a little. Then the beautiful Spaniard smiled and nodded. 'Very well. I will let you go alone. But you must bring me back scarlet ribbons and some fabric I have seen in a catalogue. Old Tom does his best, but cannot always get what I want.'

'Of course,' said Connie, overwhelmed by guilt. Sofia would never get her ribbons and fabric — unless Connie bought them and posted them to her. Yes, she would do that, and with a note explaining why she left.

No doubt Sofia would be glad to be rid of her then, but at least she would not let her new friend down too badly. It was of little comfort to her, as she planned her second escape attempt from Ocasa.

5

With her mind made up, Connie decided to enjoy her last evening in Ocasa. Making a definite plan, and more importantly having no-one thwart it, took some weight from her mind. She had not yet properly seen the famous pink sunset, so she was excited that not only would she manage to see it before she left, but she would see it from Nate Truman's ranch overlooking the sea. She silenced a small voice which told her that the ranch and the sea were not nearly as important to the dream scenario as the man.

Knowing she was leaving allowed her to concede her attraction to him. It would never amount to anything, even if she stayed in Ocasa. A man like him could not be interested in her — especially if he found out about her deceit. But she could perhaps fool herself, on cold winter nights in whatever place she chose to settle, that — had she stayed — he might easily have become the love of her life.

It was a dream to cherish on the evening before she took a step into the unknown.

She realised, as she travelled up to the ranch with Sofia and Reverend Youlgreave, that it was the first time she had spent any length of time in the Reverend's company. Sofia had been her helpmate for the past few days, whilst the Reverend, understandably, had other concerns to deal with in his parish.

'Are we safe to travel tonight?' Sofia asked him as he drove the buggy towards the Melissa Ranch. Sofia and the Reverend sat on the front seat, whilst Connie, dressed in the yellow satin gown Sofia had altered for her, sat sideways in the buggy behind.

'Yes. Nate has been as good as his word and allowed some of his men to stand duty with other men from the town. If you look over on the cliff there, and back up towards the hills, you might just see them.' It was still light, although the sun had already started moving lower in the sky. Connie and Sofia both glanced around and saw movement in the distance. The men looked like ants from such a long way away, but knowing they were there gave some comfort to the three travellers. 'Besides,' the Reverend continued, 'Hunter hasn't been down for several days. We can only hope he's got all he needs.'

'I do not like it,' said Sofia. 'It is too quiet. We would know, would we not, if he had been arrested elsewhere?'

'I suppose so, dear. Now don't you worry.' He touched his wife's knee in a way that was both comforting and intimate, making Connie feel that she ought to look away. 'We should look on the bright side. Nate Truman has thrown off his customary reserve and invited us to dinner. I can't think why.' The Reverend sounded amused.

'No, no, neither can I,' answered Sofia, her shoulders trembling slightly with laughter.

'Has he really never invited anyone?' asked Connie.

'No,' said the Reverend. 'Well, I tell a lie. I think he has invited Sister Alice up there. He's a benefactor of the orphanage, so I imagine it was simply to talk business. But the rest of us have waited for years. A few of us called on him when he first moved to the area, but whilst he was polite enough, he made it clear he didn't expect us to be regular visitors. We're very neighbourly around here, so it upset a few people. But he's a good man, works hard, employs a lot of the local men who'd struggle to find work otherwise, so we have come to accept that he is the way he is and none of us can change that. At least, not until now.'

'Perhaps he realises that with Hunter attacking the town, neighbours do need to stick together more,' suggested Connie.

'Yes,' the Reverend glanced around at her momentarily and she saw the trace of a smile on his lips. 'That must be it, Mrs Bradford.'

The ranch was not what Connie expected. They travelled through an avenue of orange trees, in full bloom, up the main house which stood near to the end of the cliff. It was more of a colonial-style mansion, facing out to the sea, although it was clear that the rear external area on the land side was a place of work. Cattle grazed in nearby fields, horses whinnied in their corrals, and hay bales and all manner of tools used in the keeping of cattle lay around the yard.

About two hundred yards from the main house was a bunkhouse, where a couple of men sat on the porch drinking from pewter flagons of beer, and talking quietly to each other.

'Welcome,' said Nate, helping first Sofia, then Connie down from the buggy. He was dressed in black again, but his suit collar had a fine silver braid running through it and he wore a crisp white shirt beneath a dark red waistcoat. 'I asked my cook, Maria, to hold off dinner until after the sunset. I thought Mrs Bradford might miss it again otherwise.'

Connie blushed. 'I did travel rather a long way over many months,' she said defensively.

'Yes, I know. I'm just teasing you, Mrs Bradford. Come on in. I've had some wine cooling.'

'Not for me, gracias,' said Sofia. 'Some women drink when they are with child, but not me.'

'Of course not.' Nate bowed his head gallantly and smiled. 'There's pink lemonade. To match the sunset. I suggest we go around to the front of the house and up onto the balcony. I've had drinks placed up there.'

They followed him around to the front, and Connie couldn't help but pause and look out over the ocean. Where the land curved, she could see distant snow-topped mountains. Below them, to her surprise, was the orphanage, with steps leading down from the Melissa Ranch to it. She had not noticed it whilst at the orphanage.

'Some of the older children come here to learn work skills,' Nate explained, as if catching her train of thought.

'I did not know that,' said Sofia, before Connie could answer. 'Did you know that, Christopher?'

Her husband shook his head. 'No, it's news to me — though I did wonder if the nuns were teaching them to lasso a steer when I saw one of the young men do it perfectly at the last county fair.'

'Up there,' said Nate, gesturing to a wooden staircase on the outside of the house that led to a balcony on the second storey. His gesture suggested the subject was closed, so no one pressed him for further details. In reality, Connie longed see inside the mansion, but it would have been rude to suggest it, so she followed Sofia up the steps, in turn followed by the Reverend and Nate.

'We should have another fair,' said

Sofia, when they were all settled with their drinks, awaiting the sunset. 'We do so little in this town, and I think it would be good for everyone after all the problems.'

'Good idea,' answered Nate. 'We could invite businessmen from out of the town and suggest they invest here. I could see Ocasa growing into a prosperous town. We already have the orange-growing, but it needs more industry.'

'You should come to the town committee meetings and we can talk about it, Nate,' said the Reverend. 'Your thoughts as a businessman would be welcome.'

'Perhaps I will. It's time, I guess, that I took more interest in Ocasa. I've lived here for a good part of my life, yet . . . '

'What?' Sofia and the Reverend spoke together, and both looked at him with amazement.

'I thought you only just came here about five years ago,' said the Reverend.

'No.' Nate shook his head. 'I returned

five years ago. I was born not far from here and brought up in the orphanage.'

'But you are not much older than I,' said Sofia, puzzled, 'yet I do not remember you.'

'I left when I was fifteen years old.'

'But still I would have known you,' said Sofia. 'From school, at least.'

'I was lucky enough to have a private tutor,' said Nate. 'Sister Alice was very good to me back then and recognised what she called my potential. She asked a retired minister — this was before you arrived, Reverend — to come and help me to study.'

'You went on to law school,' said Connie, who had been silent until that time. 'Sister Alice mentioned today that one of the boys got a scholarship. It was you, wasn't it?'

Nate nodded. 'That's right. So I guess it looks like all my deep, dark secrets are out.'

As he said it, Connie had the sense that he was holding something back. In reality, he had told them very little. He was brought up in the orphanage, and he studied law. There was no mention of who his family might have been, or why he was no longer a lawyer.

'Your input on the town committee would indeed be welcome,' said the Reverend. 'We do our best, but we're not too clear on all the different laws and by-laws — especially as so few of them are written in clear English.'

'I don't practise any more,' said Nate with a finality that suggested yet another discussion had come to an end. He drew in a breath. 'And, if you don't mind me saying, Reverend, the people here can't make up their minds what they want. On the one hand, they want Ocasa to be a civilised town where businesses thrive and the law is decided by the lawmakers, and on the other hand they want hired guns to come and chase off — even kill — the bad guys. But they can't have it both ways. They have to decide. It's either one or the other.

'Because once you let the hired guns

come in, you can forget civilisation. It'll just go back to being a frontier town, where the law is decided by whoever has the most guns.'

The Reverend nodded. 'I understand what you're saying, Nate. And I tend to agree with you. I'm sure no one wants to kill Hunter and his men. Just scare them off. People are frightened, and at the moment they are a million miles from all authority. As we discussed the other day, the US Marshalls won't be here for another two weeks or more. Who knows what might happen before then?'

'We have to hope that his current silence continues. Or that he's grown tired of Ocasa and moved on. Not that I'd wish it on another town.'

Whilst Connie was fascinated by the discussion, she noticed that whilst the two men were talking, the sun had begun to set. She moved to the balustrade and looked out onto a pink sky unlike anything she had ever seen. It was not just the sky, but the very air around her that became enveloped in a rose-coloured glow. It would be easy to believe that the rose-coloured glow might extend to her life. That she could blot out the lie she had told, and live happily in this beautiful place.

'Mrs Bradford has remembered why we're here,' said Nate, who appeared to have moved in very close behind her. She was certainly aware of his proximity. His breath moved a wisp of her hair, sending a shiver of delight through her.

'I remember the first time I saw this sky,' he went on. 'I was six years old and had just moved to the orphanage. I thought my life was over, but this sky convinced me that maybe it was just beginning.' She heard him laugh gently. 'Well — if I'm totally honest, I think Sister Alice might also have had something to do with that thought. I'm sure I wasn't thinking that clearly at the time.'

Sofia and the Reverend, as if by some design, had moved to the other end of the balcony.

'How did you lose your parents?' The question was out before Connie could stop herself.

'My mother died when I was five, my father when I was six.'

She was aware that he had not really answered her question. His voice had acquired the same final note it always did if he felt someone was getting too close to the real man.

'I guess,' he continued softly, 'that the pink sunset reminds you that life is bigger than we know it. We all have our own, small concerns, but out there is a world where anything can happen. Even a sky that turns the colour of a rose.'

'It's a little bit overwhelming,' said Connie in a small voice. 'Don't you think? Because we all want that small place in the world where we feel safe. The idea of walking out into the unknown . . . it's not always exciting. I remember that when we left England it seemed like an adventure — then my sister died and, suddenly, the world wasn't exciting any more. It was just terribly lonely.' She failed to stop a tear falling from her eye and rolling down her cheek.

Connie didn't know what was wrong with her. She had wanted to enjoy this sunset with the handsome man who stood behind her, yet it only served to remind her that she would never see him, or it, again. She drew in a deep breath and tried to be more casual. She hastily brushed the tear away, pretending it was a fly. She was glad that he would not have seen it from his position.

'What causes the sky to turn pink?' she asked. 'Just in case the children ask me.'

'It's something to do with the air from the sea meeting the air from the mountains. That's as far as I know,' said Nate. 'I'm not very scientific.' She felt his hand on her bare shoulder, where her shawl had slipped down. 'But it's supposed to make you feel better, not worse. You're certainly not supposed to cry. At least, not tears of sadness.'

It occurred to Connie that if he knew why she felt bad, he perhaps would not care about her emotions.

'I suppose I'm still grieving and wishing she could have seen it too.'

'Yes, I understand that. When my sister . . . ' She could not see him, but sensed rather than saw that he clamped his mouth shut. 'Let's go and eat before Maria protests that her food has gone cold.'

It was the first time he had mentioned having a sister, and Connie longed to ask him about her, but as always he pulled some unseen shutters down. He led them through the French doors, then down a curved staircase in the centre of a grand hallway. The house was furnished tastefully, though clearly the home of a man, with dark wood panelling and dim rooms off the hallway. The dining room was bright and cheerful, but showed signs of little use. It smelled slightly musty, though not unpleasantly so.

'I never use this room,' Nate

explained, as he helped Sofia and Connie into their seats. 'So you'll have to forgive me if it smells a little stale. I generally eat in the kitchen with Maria or down at the bunkhouse with the men.'

'You will have to hold a ball,' said Sofia. 'Did I not see a ballroom off to the other side?'

'Yes, you did. I meant to . . . ' He paused. 'I've always meant to hold a ball here, but never got around to it. Maybe you could advise me who to invite, Senora Youlgreave.'

Sofia was clearly thrilled with being given the task. Whilst they ate, she reeled off the names of some local businessmen and their wives, and other ranchers, as well as some young men and women who would enjoy the chance to dance.

'We could combine the two,' she chirruped happily. 'The county fair and the ball. But we must wait until the bambino is here, otherwise I cannot dance.'

'Oh, I'm not sure I can allow the mother of my child to dance the night away in any case,' said the Reverend with a gleam in his eye.

'You were not so choosy when we met at the county fair ten years ago,' retorted Sofia. 'Except that you would not allow anyone else to dance with me.'

'That still stands, considering you're even more beautiful now than you were then.'

'Shall we leave you two alone?' said Nate, grinning.

'You must forgive us,' said Sofia. 'We know it is not fashionable for an old married couple to be in love, but we never were fashionable, were we, querido?'

'My parents were in love forever too,' said Connie, dreamily.

'Yes, I remember,' said the Reverend. 'I was a little bit in love with your mother myself. That's why I had to run away to America.' He winked to show he was joking.

'But she was not the married woman that . . . ' said Sofia, who stammered when she remembered Connie was in the room.

'No!' The Reverend laughed. 'No, I can assure you, and Mrs Bradford, that her mother was devoted to Charles Ruddick.'

'She was a dreadful woman,' said Sofia. 'The married woman who pursued my Christopher. Not your wonderful mama, querida,' she said hastily to Connie.

'Yes, dear, but perhaps your usual candour is best saved for when we're alone.'

'I say what I think and feel,' said Sofia, waving her hands expressively. Connie was beginning to wonder what was in the pink lemonade, as Sofia was very animated. 'You knew that when you married me, Christopher. It is in my blood. You English, you are too reserved about your feelings. Me, I am completely open and honest.'

'A little too honest sometimes.' The Reverend took a sip of wine.

They were not arguing as such. On the few occasions Connie had seen them together, the Reverend and his wife shot sparks off each other in the same way, before dissolving into laughter. She had never seen a married couple behave in such a way in public, and once she had conquered her initial embarrassment, found it refreshing.

Judging by Nate's face, he was certainly highly amused by the whole exchange, too.

'Honesty is important,' said Sofia, warming to her theme. 'It is all we have, the truth. I do not like dishonest people. I do not like liars. Or those silly women in the town who pretend to like each other whilst digging their claws in behind their backs.' Sofia paused to draw breath and as if something else had just occurred to her. 'But I do not condemn when those I love make mistakes. Never do I do that.'

'I know you don't, darling,' said the Reverend.

'Well,' said Nate, 'now we've got that

clear and dinner is almost over, what do we do now? I gather, Mrs Bradford, that in your country the ladies would retire to the drawing room whilst the men smoke cigars and drink port.'

Connie smiled. 'We didn't move in those sort of circles. When Mama and Papa had a dinner party, we all retired to the drawing room and talked together. Mama always said it was silly to separate men and women as if they were from different species. But, of course, it's up to you, as our host.'

He smiled warmly. 'I must say I agree with your mama.'

6

Nate showed them to the drawing room, which had a roaring fire. Ocasa turned very cold in the evenings, despite the searing heat of the daytime sun.

Like the dining room, the drawing room showed little sign of use and Connie suspected it had been opened up especially for their visit. She could smell dust burning as it fell onto the fire and candelabras.

Above the fireplace was a portrait of a pretty, fair-haired young woman, dressed in white and wearing a summer bonnet. Her presence filled the room and hung heavily in the air.

'This is your wife, si?' asked Sofia, gazing up at the oil painting. Once again Connie blessed her outspoken friend for daring to ask what no one else would.

'No, she's my sister.'

'And she was called Melissa,' said Connie, softly.

'That's very perceptive of you, Mrs Bradford. Again. She was indeed called Melissa. Please sit down, everyone, and make yourself comfortable. I'll go and ask Maria where the coffee is.'

She couldn't miss the pain in his voice when he said his sister's name.

Connie, Sofia and the Reverend took their seats, as they had been bidden. When Nate returned, bearing a tray of coffee cups, even the normally voluble Sofia was too tactful to ask what had happened to his sister. There was no real need. The answer seemed to hang in the air with the dust and her presence.

After an awkward silence, which Connie felt sure was due to the portrait, the talk turned once again to Hunter and his group of bandits.

'This may sound naïve,' said Connie, 'but has anyone ever tried to talk to this man Hunter? To offer him and his men work in the town? I was only thinking yesterday that no one needs to steal from Ocasa. You all offer your help to others freely.'

'For some people, it isn't about stealing just to fill their bellies,' said Nate darkly. 'It's about the thrill of the chase and, I guess, stolen fruit tasting the sweetest.'

'Sofia said that some people are just born bad. I'd like to believe everyone has the capacity for good. As I said, I know I sound naïve.'

'There's nothing wrong with being naïve at your age,' said Nate. 'I just hope you don't have to learn the hard way that Sofia is right.'

There was an edge to his voice that she could not ignore. Neither could she miss the glance he cast at his sister's picture when he spoke.

'Some people are born bad, and there's no way to change them.'

'Yet I have to believe in redemption,' said the Reverend. 'Even if someone starts off as a bad lot, or falls by the wayside for a short time, I have to believe that all men, and women, can redeem themselves.'

'Do you not think that there are some sins which are unforgivable?' asked Connie tremulously.

'Yes. Of course. As an ordinary man with all the failings that go with it, I believe that some sins are unforgivable. But as a man of God, it is not for me to decide.'

'Vengeance is mine, sayeth the Lord.' Nate uttered the Scripture quotation darkly.

'An eye for an eye,' put in Sofia.

'You really believe that?' asked Nate, frowning.

'My wife is, thankfully, allowed freer views on such things,' said the Reverend, smiling. 'Although I do sometimes wish she'd save them for when we're alone.'

'Si, I believe it,' said Sofia, passionately. 'If someone hurts those I love, then I would hunt them down and destroy them, wife of a Reverend or not.' She snapped her fingers to illustrate her point.

Nate's face froze, and the atmosphere in the room became charged with electricity. 'As your husband states,' Nate eventually said in a tightly controlled voice, 'it is for God to decide. Or the law. Can you imagine a world where everyone set out to destroy the people who hurt them? It would be a world of anarchy and destruction. I'm not sure I'd want to live in such a world. That's why we have laws.' He took in a deep, cleansing breath and smiled, breaking the tension. 'But remind me never to get on the wrong side of you, Senora Youlgreave.'

'I am sure you could not do that, Senor.' Sofia gave him her most charming smile.

'I wonder . . . ' murmured Connie, feeling as if her dress constricted her and wondering what Sofia would say if she knew how Connie had abused her husband's trust. ' . . . if I could go back up to the balcony, for some air?' She stood up, longing to flee the room, but remembering her manners just in time.

'Of course, we shall come with you,' said Nate. He stood up and followed her to the door.

'You two go,' said Sofia, with a conspiratorial wink at her husband. 'We will drink our coffee. I do not think it is good for me to keep climbing all those stairs.'

A few moments later, Connie stood overlooking the bay and breathing deeply, trying to ease the constriction in her chest.

'She's a woman of . . . erm . . . how can I put this? Great passion. Senora Youlgreave, I mean.' Nate leaned forward and rested his hands on the balustrade next to her.

'Yes. It's certainly never dull, spending time in her company,' said Connie, trying to smile.

'And yet, for all her fiery words — I don't believe she could hurt a fly.'

'No — you're probably right. She's

been wonderful to me. It's like having an older sister again.'

Connie gasped, realising what she had said, but she was prevented from covering her mistake by the sound of shouts from below them.

'Nate!' A man, whom Connie guessed was one of the ranch hands, stood in shadow, below the balcony. 'Nate, we just got word. The night-time mail train has been hijacked about ten miles to the north. We think it was Hunter and his men.'

'Dear God! Is anyone hurt?'

'They blew up the track, Nate. The train was derailed and . . . they say it's real bad.'

The man paused, and Connie guessed straight away that he had even worse news. 'Nate — they say some of the US Marshalls were on it.'

'Damn! I'm on my way.'

'I'll come with you,' said Connie quickly. 'I have some nursing skills, such as they are.'

Nate looked at her for a long

moment, then nodded. She was not sure because the light was dim, but he seemed pleased with her decision. 'Okay. You go and tell the Reverend and Sofia where we're going, I'll meet you out front. We may need the Reverend, but I think Senora Youlgreave should stay here.'

'I think that might be difficult to achieve. She'll want to help, too.'

'Yeah, I know, but we can't risk having a heavily pregnant woman out there amongst the carnage. We'll have more than enough to deal with.'

Connie nodded her agreement. He was right, of course — but convincing Sofia of that would not be easy.

In the end it was the Reverend who had the last word against a protesting Sofia. 'My love,' he said in a domineering tone that Connie had never heard. 'I realise you wish to help, but I am ordering you to stay here. If you go into labour whilst we're there, who can take care of you? I hate to say it, dear, but you'll only be in the way. Now stay here with Maria. Ask her if there's anywhere you can rest.'

Sofia began to protest in a volley of Spanish mixed with English.

'You are not coming and that's that,' replied the Reverend calmly.

'Si, si. You are my husband and I suppose I must obey you,' said Sofia in sulky tones.

'Yes, you must. At least just this once. Tomorrow you can go back to completely ignoring anything I say.'

Sofia smiled. 'I do not ignore you. I listen, and then do as I please.' She turned to Connie. 'Querida, you must remember everything that happens and all the details of the hijack to tell me when you return. Men, they are not good with such details.'

'I will,' said Connie. Despite the seriousness of the situation it was hard not to smile at Sofia's desire for all the gory details.

* * *

'I wonder why the US Marshalls came sooner,' mused the Reverend as they drove at break-neck speed towards the scene of the crash. Other men from the town had joined them on the road, creating a convoy of rescue vehicles. Some of the wives had come, too. It occurred to Connie that Sofia would be upset about that, but Nate had been right to make her stay away. The ride was a bumpy one, and might easily have brought on an early labour.

'I asked them to come,' said Nate. 'I wired an old friend in the State Department the other day, to see if I could speed things up a little, but I didn't want to say anything in case they couldn't come. Damn it! I might have brought them to their deaths.' He turned a little to look at Connie, who sat behind them, clinging onto a small case full of medical equipment and trying hard not to fall off the seat as the buggy rattled and bumped over the uneven landscape. 'I apologise for my language, Mrs Bradford. That's twice

I've cussed in front of you. You too, Reverend.'

'I'm not offended,' said Connie immediately. 'There are worse things to worry about tonight.'

'I agree,' said the Reverend. 'Do we know if there are any fatalities?'

Nate shook his head. 'No, but I guess we'll soon find out.'

'How long has it been since the crash?'

'I don't know,' said Nate. 'A couple of hours, maybe. Curly, my ranch hand, said that a stagecoach was in the area and saw what happened, then rushed to Ocasa to raise the alarm. Hunter would know that even if someone sent for help, it would be some time coming. The nearest town in the other direction is thirty miles.'

The carnage, when they reached the crash site some time later, was like nothing Connie had ever seen or wanted to see again. Some of the guards and passengers who had not been badly injured had managed to hook up some lanterns.

Bodies lay strewn around the ground. Some moved slightly and emitted groans of pain. Some, most chillingly, made no sound at all.

Nate spoke to one of the guards, who filled them in on the situation. The man was trembling as he spoke, still clearly in shock but trying to hold it together to help the others.

'We weren't expecting anything like this. We heard an explosion, then the next thing you know, the train is off the rails. It happened too fast for us to react to it, and by the time we'd all regained our faculties, the bandits had taken off with the contents of the mail carriage.'

The man paused for breath, his words having come out in a rush as if he was eager to get his story told and the ordeal over with.

'We got two US Marshalls dead, another three of the deputies injured. One of our guards died. The driver is in a bad way. If this had been daytime, it might have been much worse. Though if you ask me, Mr Truman, it's bad enough. But we only had about twenty passengers, including the marshalls, three guards and the driver. We just unloaded some folks at the last town, some thirty miles north of here.'

Instinctively Connie went to an elderly woman, who was sitting up against a carriage, holding a trembling hand to her head. She was leaning on the roof, on account of the carriage having rolled onto its side.

'Where are you hurt?' Connie asked gently. She held a lantern up to the woman's face.

'Darn near everywhere,' said the woman. 'My head, is worse, Miss. It hurts real bad. I think I cut it.'

'Let me see.'

The woman had a gash in her head, but as far as Connie could see it did not go too deep. She cleaned the wound as best she could and put a dressing on it. She also checked the woman for other injuries. There were none she could see externally, and she hoped that the aches the lady felt was more to do with her age and the sudden jolt of the train leaving the track. She imagined that would be enough to shake up anyone's body.

'We got some brandy here,' said a male voice behind her. Connie turned and saw Joshua, the man with the magnificent whiskers, whom she had first seen at the schoolhouse. 'Maybe the lady would like some to calm her nerves.'

Connie nodded. 'Thank you, Mr . . . ' She realised she didn't know his last name, tending to think of him as Billy's grandfather, after the young boy with the outlaw comic.

'Stephenson, but you can call me Joshua, Mrs Bradford. Just about everyone in these parts does.'

'Thank you, Joshua.' She helped the woman to drink some brandy, then as soon as she knew she was fairly comfortable, moved on to the next injured person. It was a young fair-haired woman, in her early twenties, and she was crying for her baby.

'I can't find him,' she sobbed.

'How old is he?' asked Connie. 'Could he have wandered off?'

'No, ma'am. He's only a babe in arms. I tried to hold onto him so tight but . . . ' The girl burst into tears. 'I couldn't. When the train crashed, I just lost hold of him.'

'I'll go and see if I can find him,' said Connie. In reality she feared the worst, but did not want to upset the girl for no reason.

'I don't think there is a baby,' said one of the woman from the town as Connie asked around. 'I think maybe the girl is just in shock. If it was alive, it'd be crying, I'm sure.'

'The guard would know,' said Connie. But the guard knew nothing about the girl. He had been the attendant in the first class carriage; the man who had attended the second class carriages was dead.

'Where is the second class carriage now?' asked Connie. 'Can you identify it to me?'

'It's that one, teetering on the track, Miss. I wouldn't go in there if I were you. It could fall at any minute. That's why we moved everyone away from it.'

She looked across and in the light of the lanterns saw the carriage half-hanging on the track, its front buckled by the force of the explosion.

'We have to find the baby,' she said, emphatically. 'Or at least satisfy ourselves it isn't in there.' She could hardly believe that the young woman's fears had been ignored, but trying to be charitable, she accepted that the shock of the crash had thrown everyone off kilter.

Without waiting to listen to an argument to the contrary, Connie headed towards the second class carriage. Even as she climbed up on the running board, she felt it move slightly and heard the sound of creaking metal. Her instinct was to flee, back to the relative safety of the others, but her humanity would not allow her to leave a child who might be in need of medical help.

'Don't go in there! Dammit, come back! You little fool!'

She was already in the small passageway leading to the carriage when she heard Nate call her, and then it took her a few seconds to realise it was her he meant, but she ignored him anyway. Holding her lantern aloft, she walked slowly through the carriage, feeling it rocking beneath her due to the imbalance she caused. Already she regretted her decision — but it was too late to go back now.

The position meant that she was walking on the sides of her feet, with her body pressed against the seats. She wished she had remembered to ask the young woman where she and her baby had been sitting.

Then she heard it. A small moan, from beneath one of the seats near the front.

Bending down, Connie shone her lantern and saw the baby. He had been thrown against the wall of the carriage. She reached under and grabbed his shawl, sliding him gently to her so as not to cause any more movement than necessary.

'Goddammit, you shouldn't be in here,' said Nate tensely from the doorway of the carriage.

'Neither should you,' she admonished. 'Shh, don't move or you'll rock the carriage. I've found the baby.'

It was all she could do not to clasp the child to her in relief when she finally held him in her arms, but she was still trying to be careful so as not to cause too much movement. She stood up and started walking slowly towards Nate. 'He's safe,' she told him, with an elated smile.

Nate shook his head incredulously, and smiled too. 'We were never going to convince you to stay out of here, were we?'

When Connie was only a few feet away from Nate, the carriage began to sway precariously. She was aware of him yanking her into his arms, crushing the baby between them, then hoisting her up and jumping from the carriage with her. They hit the ground several yards away, with a resounding thud. Before Connie had time to think, Nate had pulled her and the baby up, lifting her again, and running hell for leather, as the carriage lurched behind them, landing with an almighty crash just a few feet away from where Nate had thrown Connie to the ground, covering her and the baby with his own body.

They sat up. Connie immediately looked down at the baby.

'Is he . . .'

Before she could finish her question, the baby let out a lusty scream.

'I think he's doing fine,' said Nate. 'Or at least his lungs are.'

'I'll take him to his mama.'

'Okay, but you and I will have a talk later about walking blindly into dangerous situations.'

'Somebody had to,' Connie retorted. 'People were ready to believe his mother had imagined him rather than go and check.'

'People were trying to keep safe in

what is an already critical situation . . . Mrs Bradford.'

Connie nodded, not much liking the way he'd spat out her name. Or her sister's name. Fatigue was making her confused again.

'Yes, I know that. I'm sorry. I don't mean to criticise. I know things are bad here, but if I hadn't gone to check . . . '

'Go on, take him to his mama.'

'I'm sorry if I put anyone in danger,' murmured Connie, shame-faced.

'I wasn't thinking or worrying about anyone else.'

Without stopping to wonder what he meant by that, Connie carried the baby boy to his relieved and delighted mother.

'Oh, my Artie. My baby,' she sobbed, hugging the child to her. 'Thank you, Miss . . . I don't even know your name.'

Connie had to think for a moment to remember exactly who she was supposed to be. The falling carriage had destroyed her equilibrium. Though later, when she was more honest with herself, her confusion probably had more to do with the feel of Nate's body over hers as he protected her from the falling train.

'Mrs Bradford. Elizabeth Bradford. What's your name?'

'I'm Cindy-Lou Vickers and this is my son, Arthur. But I call him Artie, after his daddy. We're on our way to join his daddy, aren't we, baby?'

'Your husband lives in Ocasa?'

There was a noticeable pause. 'Yes. Or thereabouts. He doesn't know I'm coming. He doesn't even know about Artie. They say being a daddy changes a man. Do you think that's true, Mrs Bradford?'

'I'm afraid I don't have much experience in such matters,' said Connie apologetically. 'But I know I had the most wonderful father in the world.'

'That's how all little girls feel about their daddies. It's how I felt about mine . . . only now . . . ' Cindy-Lou shook her head. 'I don't wanna think about that. And I'm keeping you from helping others.'

In reality, there was not much more

to do. With so many men and women there from the town, the injured were cared for almost on a one-to-one basis. Connie went to offer help where she could.

The next few hours were spent arranging for those who were most badly injured to be carried back to the town first, so they could receive medical treatment. The walking wounded travelled back with the rest of the townspeople, all of whom had agreed to put them up. Nate suggested that Cindy-Lou and baby Artie travel back with them, offering them a room at his ranch. He also insisted that the Reverend, Sofia and Connie stay over, to save them the trip back into town.

Only much later, as the sun was beginning to rise again, and Connie retired, exhausted, to bed at the Melissa Ranch, did her eyes snap open with a startling realisation. With the train track buckled and no hope of a quick repair, her escape route had been closed to her.

7

The days passed by in a sultry glow, and before Connie knew it, she was teaching at the school and over a week had passed by since the train crash. She had not given up entirely her idea of leaving. But she had put it to the back of her mind. Something to think about late at night, whenever the enormity of the lie she had told caught up with her.

Cindy-Lou and baby Artie had remained up at Melissa Ranch, something Connie admitted to feeling envious about. Several times she saw Cindy-Lou and Nate together in the town, and saw the admiration with which the girl gazed up at him. She wondered, with an ache in her heart, whether Nate was falling in love with the young mother. His attitude towards the girl seemed little more than proprietary — the same gentlemanly way in which he treated all women — but Cindy-Lou was very young and very pretty.

She did notice that neither she, Sofia nor the Reverend were invited to Melissa Ranch again, but it would have been strange indeed had a man who had closed himself off from the world for so long suddenly opened his doors to neighbours every night. At least, that was what Connie hoped. She cast aside a niggling idea that it was because he was enjoying Cindy-Lou's company too much.

Connie had not had much chance to talk to him, but one afternoon after school, they were once again thrown together in difficult circumstances — albeit not as life-threatening as the train crash.

The day had started well. Billy Estevez, Sofia's nephew and the young man with a fixation on outlaws, had befriended Bernardo, the boy from the orphanage. Connie hoped that the friendship would benefit Bernardo as Billy was from a good, honest family, but a conversation she overheard in the morning dismayed her.

She had split the class into two groups. The younger children were set to learn their ABCs, with the help of one of the teenage Senoritas who had offered her services as a classroom assistant because she too hoped to be a teacher one day. The older children were studying science.

'If I say to you that what goes up must come down, of what am I speaking?' asked Connie, standing in front of the older group.

She looked at a sea of frightened faces. The children exchanged glances, clearly wondering who was going to be the first to look a fool by getting it wrong.

'It doesn't matter if you're wrong,' she said with an encouraging smile. 'People learn more by their mistakes than when they get things right.'

'It's gravity,' a small voice said. Connie smiled at him.

'Well done, Bernardo. Gravity. Gravity is what keeps our feet on the ground, and what makes things we throw up in the air fall back to the ground. Do you know who discovered it?'

Bernardo shook his head. The other children looked back at her with blank expressions. She was beginning to wonder exactly what the last schoolmistress had taught them, but put it down to them still feeling a little shy in her presence.

'It was Sir Isaac Newton. As the story goes, he fell asleep under an apple tree one day and was awoken by one falling on his head. That's when he began to develop his theory of gravity. What I want you to do this morning is test this theory. I've brought tennis balls, feathers, and all manner of other, unbreakable, objects. I want you to form an orderly queue and go out into the schoolyard. Bernardo, would you like to help me carry the equipment?'

'Didn't your last teacher tell you all about gravity?' Connie asked Bernardo as she handed him the equipment from the closet.

Bernardo shook his head. 'I only came here a few weeks before she left. She was very religious. There was a man . . . I forget his name . . . but when the town committee said she should tell us about it, she refused. Then, before she married — to a travelling minister who was not as kind as Reverend Youlgreave, and who used to come and tell us we would all go to hell if we didn't give him five dollars to pray for us — she said all science was evil. For the last few weeks before she left, she only allowed us to read Bible passages. Billy just read his comics, I think, between the pages of the Bible. He says I can read them, now we are friends.'

Connie did not like that idea, but kept silent about it.

'Was it Charles Darwin who upset her?'

'Yes, that is the man. Mr Darwin. He says we are all monkeys.'

'That's not exactly what he says,' said Connie, making a mental note to explain it properly to the children when she had the chance.

'That is what Sister Alice said. Sister Alice said that even science is God's creation, so we should not fear it. She says that to ignore it is more dangerous.'

'Sister Alice is very wise.'

Bernardo nodded. 'Mrs Bradford?'

'What, dear?'

'I knew that it was Newton who invented gravity. But I did not like to say, as the other boys laugh at me and call me teacher's pet.'

'First of all,' Connie said gently, 'Newton didn't *invent* gravity. It was already there. More importantly, you should never pretend to be anything other than what you are, Bernardo.'

As she uttered the words, she was aware of the irony of her voicing that opinion, and hoped Bernardo was not so smart as to notice her blushes. 'You're a clever boy, and it doesn't matter what others think. So if you know the answer to something, you shout it out. Is that a deal?'

Bernardo nodded and gave one of his smiles, which somehow still managed to look a little sad. 'Sister Alice said you would be a good teacher. She said she could tell.'

'We'd better get these things outside, or I shan't be that good a teacher,' said Connie. 'Come along.'

She turned, and saw Nate Truman standing a few feet away.

'Ma'am.' He nodded.

'Good morning, Mr Truman. We didn't hear you come in.'

'You were deep in conversation.' Something in his expression told her that he approved. This made her feel all hot and flustered. She put it down to the heat of the day.

'I called in to ask if you would like to join us up at the Ranch for dinner tonight. Cindy-Lou is eager to see you again.'

'I . . . er . . . I'm sorry, I can't.' If he hadn't mentioned Cindy-Lou, she might have said yes. She hurried on, 'I'm moving into my own cottage at the weekend, and I'm going up there most evenings to clean it up and make it ready. Perhaps some other time.'

Nate nodded, his eyes narrowing slightly. 'Bernardo,' he said in friendly tones to the child, 'why don't you take those things outside for Mrs Bradford?'

When Bernardo had gone, Nate looked around and saw the Senorita was absorbed in her work with the younger children. He spoke softly.

'If this is about the way I criticised you on the night of the train crash, then I'm really sorry about that. I was merely concerned about you.'

'Oh, no. It's not that. I really do have to sort the cottage out. Some of Mr Stephenson's . . . Joshua's . . . men have mended the roof for me, and I want to finish painting. I've imposed on Sofia and the Reverend for long enough. Especially with the baby due.'

'I'm sure they'd be happy to put up with you, as you say, for longer. They're very fond of you.'

'I'm very lucky and very grateful,' she

said, casting her eyes down briefly, knowing she did not deserve their kindness. 'But I would like a place of my own, with my own front door.'

She did not want to seem ungrateful, but Sofia's almost maternal ministrations felt quite overpowering at times. Connie could hardly move without Sofia wanting to know where she was going.

She already loved the Reverend's wife as if she were a sister, but nevertheless she felt constricted. Perhaps it had more to do with her knowing that she was lying to Sofia than with any real fault on the emotional and naturally caring Spaniard's part.

'She cares about you a lot,' said Nate, as if he had read Connie's thoughts. 'Senora Youlgreave. I know she's a bit of a mother hen, but you are all alone here. What worries me is that, if you go and live in the schoolmistress's cottage, you'll be lonelier still. It is some way out of town. I gather the last schoolmistress moved into a room above Old

Tom's store because she didn't like being out there.'

'Is it true she married a travelling preacher?'

Nate smiled. 'Oh, yeah. A really interesting guy. All hellfire and brimstone and 'give me all your money or you're going to hell'. Thankfully she was the only one really taken in by him. But you're not changing the subject on me here. Please, think before you move into that cottage. It's secluded, and a long way from help.'

'Joshua has set up a warning triangle above the door,' Connie replied. 'If anything happens I'm to bang on it. It can be heard from the town.'

'I can't hear it where I am,' said Nate, pointedly.

'I'll get a bigger triangle,' returned Connie, laughing. 'Besides, won't Hunter and his men have moved on by now? That's what everyone is saying, since he got what he wanted from the mail train.'

Nate shook his head. 'I'm afraid it's not that simple. The mail train was carrying just that. Mail. He may have found a dollar or two tucked inside some of the letters, but it won't be enough to buy him and his men more than a few beers in any saloon crazy enough to serve them.'

'So it's not over,' mused Connie. Then suddenly her thoughts returned to the present. 'Oh! — I'm sorry, I really ought to get to the children.'

She dashed out into the playground. She knew she had been very remiss in leaving them outside on their own, but Nate had a distracting effect on her. Maybe it was the same effect the hellfire and brimstone preacher had on the last teacher — but she doubted it. If that preacher knew what went through Connie's mind whenever she was in Nate's company, she would be the one going to hell.

'And,' Billy Estevez was saying to Bernardo, as they pored over his outlaw comic, 'we'll hold up a train then become desperadoes, like your daddy. Moving from place to place.'

'William Estevez,' said Connie in strict tones that sounded strange even to her. 'Give that to me this instant.'

Furious with the boy, she had to pause and remind herself he was indeed only a child. It was the mention of Bernardo's father that enraged her, along with Billy's childlike assumption that Bernardo would automatically follow suit.

'Now,' said Connie, when Billy had reluctantly handed over the book. 'I'm going to confiscate this until you go home. Then, I'm going to be speaking to your mother about making you leave these books at home. I don't care what the last teacher let you get away with because she had her mind on other things; you are not going to be reading this between the pages of your text books in my class. Is that clear?'

'Yes, Ma'am,' said Billy, with tears filling his brown eyes. He and Bernardo could easily have been brothers, they were so alike.

Connie wanted to give him a hug and

tell him it was all right, but she believed she had to nip his fantasies in the bud, for fear that one day they might move beyond that. In truth, she worried more for Bernardo — who, unlike Billy, had no good male role models in his life.

'And neither are you and Bernardo going to be holding up any trains whilst you're my students.'

She heard a laugh behind her. Nate, arms folded, looked highly amused. 'You hear that, boys,' he said. 'No holding up any trains until you've left school.'

The rest of the children laughed. Connie flashed her eyes at him furiously. She felt that he'd undermined her authority with the children.

'If you'll excuse me, Mr Truman, I have a class to teach,' she said through gritted teeth.

'Look . . . ' Nate's voice softened. He was about to say something to Connie, but instead turned to the boys. 'You two mind Mrs Bradford now, do you hear? If I find out you've misbehaved, I'm gonna tan both your hides and hang them in my yard as a warning to other boys who don't listen to their teachers.'

Billy and Bernardo nodded vehemently, whilst the other children looked on, wide-eyed. Connie wanted to laugh then, but she clamped her lips together. She sensed that he would never raise his hand to a child, but being a big man with a scar on his face, he knew that the threat would be enough.

Besides, she was angry. He had still undermined her authority, even with his threat. The boys would certainly listen to him, but whether they ever listened to her again was another matter!

It was much later in the day when she found out that even if Billy and Bernardo had been overwhelmed by Nate's powerful personality at that moment, the effect had quickly faded.

8

The children had been dismissed, and Connie looked forward to going up to her cottage before the daylight faded. She was on her way to Old Tom's to pick up some supplies, when she saw Bernardo running hell for leather out of the shop, closely followed by Billy, then Old Tom, who was waving his walking stick.

'You little varmints! Come back here. Steal from me, would yer?'

Bernardo turned in the direction of the hills, only to run straight into Nate. It would have been comical to see Bernardo's legs continuing to run in mid-air, had the situation not been so serious.

'That little . . . ' Old Tom muttered an expletive, 'stole candy from my shop! Call the sheriff.'

'Billy! Come back here this instant,'

cried Connie, as Billy tried to slip past her. She managed to grab the collar of his shirt. She pulled him over to where Nate stood with Bernardo still high up in the air.

'No need for the sheriff, Tom,' said Nate. 'Let me deal with this.'

'These orphans. I always said they'd cause trouble in this town when them nuns arrived here thirty years ago.'

'Now, you know as well as I do that that's not true, Tom,' said Nate, setting Bernardo on the ground but keeping a firm hand on him. 'The orphans are no trouble in this town. If we're going to talk about blame, what about young Billy here? Or does his grandfather being on the town committee allow him to steal from you?'

'It was that one as did it,' said Tom, spluttering and pointing to Bernardo. Connie saw from his face that Nate's words had hit home.

'And Billy was in there too, wasn't he? And ran away afterwards?'

'That's true, Mr Truman. Very true.

But maybe he was just scared at my shouting. I don't want no trouble with Joshua. If Billy's got in with a wrong crowd . . . '

'Leave this to me,' said Nate, his jaw twitching in anger. 'Bernardo, give the man his candy back and apologise.'

'I'm truly sorry, sir,' Bernardo whispered, handing back the sweets.

'Promise you'll never do it again.'

'I'll never do it again. I swear, Mr Truman.' The boy's words were barely audible.

'Good. Now. Billy, Bernardo . . . Mrs Bradford, come with me please.'

They followed him, and Connie realised he was going in the direction of the graveyard.

'What exactly did you plan to do once you'd stolen the candy?' asked Nate as they made their short journey. 'Go and live in the hills?'

'Something like that,' said Billy. 'We're gonna be desperadoes and outlaws, like Bernardo's pa.'

'Bernardo, if Billy told you to go and

jump off the cliff up at my place, would you do it?' asked Nate.

'No, sir. But . . . '

'So it was Billy's idea that you steal the candy.'

'No, sir. We both decided.' Connie admired Bernardo's loyalty to his friend, even if he was lying. When she was a schoolgirl, it had been an unspoken rule that no one told tales on a fellow student.

'Hmm,' said Nate. 'Every gang has a leader. So I'm guessing you're the leader, Bernardo. The mastermind behind this ingenious crime.'

'No, he ain't,' piped up Billy indignantly. 'I'm Jesse James. He's just one of my men.'

Nate turned to Billy, his face grim as if carved in stone. 'And do you know what one of Jesse James' men did to him, Billy? He shot him in the back. In cold blood.'

'Mr Truman,' said Connie in warning tones, feeling that Nate might be going a little bit too far.

'Mr Truman, nothing,' said Nate. 'If Billy wants to be an outlaw, he needs to know exactly what's awaiting him out there. But first I want to try something else.'

As he finished speaking they reached the graveyard. Several freshly dug mounds filled one side. 'Do you see these here graves, boys?'

Billy and Bernardo nodded, and Connie was sure they believed Nate planned to throw them into the holes.

'These here graves are for the people killed on the train. Some of them were deputy US Marshalls, and those men had wives and children waiting at home for them. Now those children are going to grow up without a pa. Billy, you don't know what that's like, because you have a pa, and a grandpa. You go home every night and see them, and they tuck you into bed, maybe read you a story or tell you about their youth. But me and Bernardo, we know what it's like not to have a father, don't we, Bernardo?'

'Si, senor.'

'And these men, these marshals, had only come here to protect you from bandits like those guys you read about in your comics, Billy. They didn't have to do that. They could have stayed at home, all safe and in the arms of their families, reading to their own children at night. But they travelled all the way across country to protect you from the kind of men you want to be. Other people died, too. Innocent people, on their way to visit their folks or to start an honest job.' Nate looked at Bernardo, with some unknown emotion in his face. 'Bernardo, do you want to tell Billy what it's really like to be the son of an outlaw, or shall I?'

Connie, who had been looking at Billy, spun round.

'I do not remember much,' said Bernardo, but it was clear from his haunted expression that he did.

'Okay,' said Nate. 'I'm guessing it still hurts. And it will hurt for a long time. So I'll tell Billy about being nearly six years old and walking for days, holding my baby sister in my arms, whilst my daddy moved from one town to another, taking whatever he could get. He said it was to feed us, and that one day we'd be rich.

'We didn't need to be rich. We just needed to be fed. He could have chopped wood, or worked the railroad. He could even have hunted for food. There's enough work and food in this big old country for any man who's not afraid of hard work. But my pa wanted the easy way of life. Not like your pa and grandpa, Billy, who work the fields from morning till night to put food in your belly. My pa wanted to simply take what others had earned by the sweat of their brow. So we'd walk for days, while the rain got into my shoes . . . until they fell apart and I had no shoes left, and I struggled to keep my baby sister warm in a blanket that was crawling with fleas because my daddy had stolen it from some dog.

'Then we'd sleep out under the stars.

Sounds exciting, don't it? Not when you're hungry and there's lizards and snakes crawling all over you, and your little baby sister is weeping beside you, it isn't.'

Connie found she was listening with as much rapt attention as the boys. She fought back the tears that stung her eyes, hearing about the hardship Nate faced and the responsibility he had felt towards Melissa.

'Then,' Nate continued, in a tone of irony fused with pain, 'if your children are really lucky, they might see you gunned down outside a bank one day. It'll give them something to dream about on lonely nights. Do you still think about that, Bernardo? I sure do.'

Bernardo nodded. 'I did not see it, but I . . . I see it anyway. In dreams.'

'I know, son. But you're smarter than your pa. Just because he was your pa, you don't have to be the same as he was, no matter what Billy tells you. It's what's in your heart that matters, not what's in your blood. Remember what Mrs Bradford said to you in class this morning. You be the person you're supposed to be. I can tell, and I know she can tell, that you're supposed to be a good man. Women are nearly always right, you know. That's something I've learned in my life. Sister Alice, Mrs Bradford, Senora Youlgreave. They're the ones you should heed. Billy!'

'Yes, sir . . . ' Billy's bottom lip was trembling as he jumped to attention.

'Does your mama tell you to be good?'

'Yes, sir.'

'Then you mind her in future. You don't wanna grow up to be shot in the back by someone you thought was your friend, do you?'

'N . . . no, sir.'

'I'm gonna be talking to your pa and grandpa and telling them I don't think you should be reading those comics any more. You're not smart enough yet to realise that they're pretend. Maybe more time in Mrs Bradford's class will teach you better. I sure hope so.'

'You're not really going to tan our hides, are you, sir?' asked Billy, starting to cry.

'I'm sure thinking of it at this moment because I'm angry with you both for being so stupid. But everyone deserves a second chance, so I'm giving you one. If I hear you've stolen from Old Tom or anyone else in this town again, I'll be out looking for you both.' His mouth twitched slightly, but his words had the desired effect. 'One more thing, Billy.'

'Yes, sir.'

'You're to own up to Old Tom and your folks that you had a part in this theft. It ain't fair that Bernardo takes all the blame. He was loyal to you, now you've got to be loyal to him. That's what a real man does when his back's against the wall. He stands by his friends.'

'Yes, sir.'

'And,' said Nate, pointedly, 'a real man never asks his friend to do something he's not prepared to do himself.

That doesn't make him a criminal mastermind. It makes him a coward who's afraid of getting his own hands dirty. Do I make myself clear?'

'Yes, sir.'

'Good. Then we're done here. Run on home, both of you. I'll be talking to your folks later, Billy, and to Sister Alice, Bernardo.'

'Perhaps I should be the one talking to them,' said Connie as the boys ran out of the churchyard.

'No offence, Mrs Bradford,' said Nate, 'but men like Billy's pa and grandpa don't take much notice of womenfolk.'

'What about Sister Alice?'

'Yeah, she'll listen to you. But not tonight. Let Bernardo tell her himself. It'll be good for him.'

'You speak from experience?'

'Yep. I was wild as a coyote when I first arrived at the orphanage. I was angry at the world, and determined to have my revenge. Sister Alice soon cured me of that.'

'I'm sorry about your father.'

'Don't be.' Nate had closed off again, perhaps because the pain of remembering was too much.

'I'm worried about Billy,' said Connie. 'I think he's listening to you, because you're bigger and stronger than he is and talked louder. But . . . ' Connie spread her hands as if the dangers were too big to explain.

Nate nodded. 'Yeah, he's got problems. The main one being that his family have indulged him too much.'

'Are you saying that they're wrong to tuck him in and tell him stories every night?'

'No, of course not. But they haven't taught him enough about real life in between telling him the stories. There's nothing wrong with a child having an imagination. But he doesn't know the difference between what's real and what's pretend and because he makes them laugh with his wild imaginings, he laughs back. He doesn't know there are limits.'

'I have an idea that might help — I'll get him writing his own stories. When I was little, I had a vivid imagination too. If I read something in a book, I would believe every word, often frightening myself in the process. My mother encouraged me to write all my day-dreams down. It helped to expunge them a little, because I knew for myself that what I'd written on the page wasn't real. Hopefully it will do the same for Billy.'

'You're going to make someone a fine mother one day, Mrs Bradford.'

Connie blushed. She had been thinking that Nate would be a good father one day, but was too shy to say so.

'You know — don't you — that the boys might well tell everyone about your father?'

'It's no secret.'

'I think it is. Or it has been. If Sofia knew, she most certainly would have told me about that.'

'Anyone could have found out if

they'd asked around other towns.'

'But now they'll know it for certain. I wouldn't like to think that . . . ' Connie stopped.

'That they'd judge me by what my pa did? Why do you think I've done my very best to live an honest life? It's so that no one could ever say that about me.'

'I'm sure they wouldn't anyway. Is that how you got your scar? Whilst travelling with your father?'

'No. That was something different. From a time when I forgot I wasn't my pa. Now I think you'd best go and get your chores done, before you lose the light.'

Connie was acutely aware of being dismissed, and that she had pressed a little too hard with her question.

'I'm sorry, I didn't mean to pry.'

'Yes, you did. It's what people do.'

'What I mean was . . . I wouldn't have told anyone, if you'd told just me. I . . . ' She faltered. 'Yes, you're right, I'd better go and do my chores.'

She walked away from him feeling despondent. She had almost got to know the real man. She certainly understood, now, the child he had been. But there was definitely something else that Nate Truman did not want to share. Something about forgetting he was not his father.

Had he robbed a bank?

She hoped not. She was forced to admit that, like Billy, she had built Nate up to be an almost mythical figure — but not in the same way. She saw him as powerful, morally sound and steadfast, and his story about carrying his baby sister and trying to keep her warm only reinforced her vision. She told herself that if he had robbed a bank, perhaps he had only done it to feed his sister — but she remembered what he had told the boys about there being plenty of employment in America for a man not afraid of hard work. That was the man she wanted him to be.

* * *

Lost in thought, Connie reached Old Tom's store without realising. She was just in time to hear him say to a customer, 'Oh yeah, Caleb Truman. I remember him. Sheriff shot him when he robbed a bank not far north of here. Must have been nigh on twenty-five years ago. It was before the railroad came to all the way down to Ocasa, I know that. So . . . ' Tom sucked on his pipe and rocked his chair in a gleeful movement. 'He's Caleb Truman's boy, is he? Who'd'a' thought it?' After another suck on his pipe, he intoned sagely, 'Bad blood runs deep. That's all I'm saying. Bad blood runs deep.'

Connie's heart sank. Billy and Bernardo had evidently wasted no time in telling everyone about Nate. She hoped it would not mean that the other townspeople would now treat him differently. He may have said that it was not a secret, but neither had he gone out of his way to tell anyone.

And why should he? Caleb was not his father in any meaningful sense, no matter what Tom said.

She fought the instinct to go and tell Tom he was wrong about Nathan, but what good would it do? She had also kept the truth from the townsfolk — and after Tom's reaction to Nathan's revelation, she feared what might happen if they ever found out the truth about her.

Nathan had done nothing illegal in Ocasa. After five years, he was a respected citizen who had proven himself to be an honest, hard-working man. She was a stranger who had arrived in the town and immediately fallen into deceiving everyone. She might not be so lucky.

She had intended to buy some supplies from Tom's store, but decided against it for fear of being asked questions about Nate. The boys would undoubtedly have mentioned she was there when Nate revealed the truth about his father.

As if to illustrate her guilt, as she passed by the bank she saw Mr Fletcher, the manager, rushing out to accost her.

She had almost forgotten about the papers he wanted her to sign, so was dismayed to see what appeared to be those very papers clutched in his hand.

'Mrs Bradford.' Mr Fletcher tipped his cap. 'I sure hope you're feeling recovered now.'

'Yes, thank you, Mr Fletcher. Only I'm in a hurry. I need to prepare my cottage, ready for the weekend.'

'It'll only take a moment, Mrs Bradford — then you can be on your way. I daresay you'll be wanting some pretty baubles for that cottage of yours, though it might be hard to get them with the railroad all broken. Oh dear, that was a dreadful tragedy, was it not?' Fletcher took his handkerchief from his top pocket and wiped his brow.

'Yes, dreadful.'

'And it leaves us cut off, unless folks travel in the overland coach, which isn't too comfortable in this heat.'

'No, I can imagine.' Connie, who had lived in an English village only half an hour's ride from the nearest big town, could not really imagine, although she was beginning to understand just how big her new home was. 'Really I must be . . . '

'Talk to you a moment, Mr Fletcher?'

Nate's brusque tone startled Connie. She had not realised he had followed her, and immediately wondered whether he had overheard Old Tom's uncharitable words.

'Mr Truman.' Fletcher tipped his hat. 'Always good to see you, Sir.' Fletcher had started sweating visibly, and Connie guessed that he too had heard the gossip. By the time she got to Sofia's, her friend would no doubt be eager for more information. Maybe Connie would go straight up to her cottage after all.

'Don't worry, Mr Fletcher, I'm not planning on robbing your bank.'

Fletcher had the grace to look ashamed. 'No, no, I'm sure you wouldn't, Mr Truman. Why, I was only saying a few moments ago, 'Mr Truman is an honest, upstanding citizen of this town, and I won't hear any different said of him.'

from the orphanage with a buggy, but no decision had yet been made, and the train derailment had turned the committee's mind to other more pressing concerns.

'True, but the children do not insist on wearing white blouses with long sleeves and thick blue skirts.'

'I hardly think the boys would anyway,' Connie said with a smile. Connie knew that she would not really be able to talk to Bernardo whilst Sofia was there, no matter how big-hearted her friend was. She decided honesty was the best policy.

'I'd really like to talk to Bernardo alone, Sofia. You understand?'

'Si, si, I understand.' Sofia looked hurt, which made Connie feel awful.

'Perhaps whilst I'm doing that you could speak to Paolo; try and make him see sense. I'm really worried about Billy. He's not a bad child, but he has a tendency to be over-imaginative and it has already got him into trouble. I fear something worse could happen.'

'Si, this is true. He is a good boy, but he does not understand the world as we do. Yes, I will speak to my brother. That is more important, I think, so this child here is not frightened any more.'

'I think so,' agreed Connie.

'Do not worry, bambino,' Sofia said to Bernardo, ruffling his hair. 'We will take care of you. You are always welcome in my house. Always. And if my brother tries to spank you, I will threaten to tell the town of all the stupid things he did as a boy.'

'Muchas gracias, Senora,' Bernardo mumbled, sniffing loudly and rewarding her with his sad smile.

'When you return,' Sofia said to Connie, 'you must tell me all you know about Nate Truman's bank robber papa. Is it not exciting to have such a man living near us?'

Connie sighed. She was beginning to see from whom Billy had inherited his romantic nature. But at least Sofia was old enough to know that the life of a real bandit was not a good one.

* * *

A short time later, Connie and Bernardo walked along the coast road together. She had given him her handkerchief, telling him to keep it. She also gave him time to compose himself before she began to speak.

'So did Billy tell his father the truth about what happened?' she asked.

'He did. But not in the way it happened,' protested Bernardo. 'He made out like he only told me to do it as a dare and that he did not believe I would really do it. That is not how it was, Senora Bradford. I know I was wrong to take the candy. But . . . '

'I know, Bernardo.' She smiled reassuringly. 'You may not believe it, but I was young myself once.'

'Sister Alice said you are not very old now. But she said that you have an old soul.'

'Did she? Oh, well, as I was saying, I was young myself once, and I know how it feels when friends try to encourage you to do things that are wrong. It's hard to stand up to them, because you want them to be your friends — and you're afraid that if you don't do just as they say, they may stop liking you.'

Bernardo nodded vigorously, as if she had hit the nail on the head.

'But you need to be more careful, Bernardo.'

'Because of my papa.'

'Yes. I'm sorry. It's not fair, but people tend to judge children by what their parents do.'

'The sins of the fathers,' said Bernardo. 'Sister Alice said she does not believe that is true.'

'And she's right. It isn't true. But sadly some people think it is, and . . .' Connie wasn't sure exactly how to explain it to a child, but Bernardo was clever. She persevered. 'Sometimes if someone is told for long enough that they're bad, they stop bothering to be good. Then they just do what everyone expects them to do.'

Bernardo sighed. 'It is hard to be good when I want so many things.'

'What do you want, dear?'

'I want a house like Senor Truman's, and horses, and books, and . . . lots of things.'

'There's nothing wrong with wanting things. You're allowed to have dreams. You'll just have to work hard at school, and then when you're older you'll be able to find work and pay for the things you want.'

'That seems like a long time.'

'I know, dear. And you may not get all you want. But when you're older you'll probably find you want other things that don't cost money.'

'You are not going to start talking about love and girls and wives and things, are you, Senora? Sister Alice does and it is very boring.'

'You won't think so when you're older and you're gazing up at the stars thinking of some pretty girl,' Connie teased. Bernardo looked up at her and rolled his eyes. She laughed and was delighted when he joined in. He slipped his hand in hers.

'You are my favourite person, after Sister Alice. And Senor Truman.'

'I'll take that as a compliment,' responded Connie, smiling. 'Muchas gracias, Bernardo.'

On hearing her clumsy Spanish pronunciation, Bernardo burst into fits of laughter.

For the next ten minutes, Bernardo taught Connie how to pronounce certain Spanish words, along with their meanings. He clearly enjoyed being her teacher, and she felt sure he walked a little taller after a while.

Despite being late in the day, the heat was searing, and she was beginning to question the wisdom of the long walk. She would also have a three-mile walk back home as, whilst the nuns had a small buggy for their use, Connie did not want to inconvenience them.

Almost as if she had spoken a prayer, she heard the rumble of wheels, followed by, 'Hey there.'

They both turned to see Nate driving his buggy towards them.

'May I offer you a lift to the orphanage?' he inquired, pulling to a halt.

'Didn't you have business with Mr Fletcher?'

'My mistake. The accounts were fine. I bought him a drink in the saloon to soothe his ego. Then I ran into Senora Youlgreave, who said you two were heading out this way. She told me what Senor Estevez said to young Bernardo there. Come on, both of you, up on the buggy. Do you wanna sit up front with me, Bernardo? I want to talk business with you.'

Connie felt a little disappointed as she climbed into the back of the buggy. She perched inelegantly on some sacks of grain.

'Did Mrs Bradford explain it all to you, Bernardo?'

'Si, Senor. About how I must be more careful to be good.'

'And how it's easy to let your friends

push you into doing bad things.'

'Si, Senor.'

'Then I guess she's covered everything I was going to say to you. Now we can chat man to man about other things.'

'What things, Senor?'

'Are you doing good at school, Bernardo?'

Bernardo considered his academic performance. 'I . . . think so, Senor.'

'Is that true, Mrs Bradford?'

'Yes. Bernardo works very hard.'

'That's what I like to hear. But you know there are other things a man needs to learn. Just in case he can't get a job using his reading and writing skills. So how would you like to come up to my place every Saturday with the bigger boys, then me and some of the hands can teach you some ranching skills? That way, you'll always be able to put food on the table, no matter what life throws at you.'

Bernardo's eyes shone as he gazed up at Nate. 'Can I really, Senor? Will Sister Alice allow it?'

'I reckon she will if I ask her and promise not to work you too hard. And if you're with us, you won't be getting into any trouble. My men are all good, honest guys. They'll steer you right. I'll pay you, too.'

'I will do it for nothing.'

'Now that's not how you put food on the table, Bernardo. You should be paid for your hard work. But . . . ' Nate's voice became ominous. Bernardo looked terrified, as if he feared Nate might snatch it all away from him. 'You gotta keep working hard at school. If Mrs Bradford tells me you're slacking in your lessons, then I can't use you on my ranch.'

'Oh, si, Senor. I will work very hard for you and for Senora Bradford.'

'Good. One more thing.'

'Senor?'

'Billy Estevez . . . Now it's all right for you to talk to him at school, and be neighbourly, because we don't want any feuds starting, but I don't think you should be hanging around with him after school. He's not as smart as you are and is liable to lead you into trouble. Stick with people you can trust. Like Sister Alice, me and Mrs Bradford here. People who want the best for you. Till you get older and can judge folks better.'

'Si, Senor.' Bernardo nodded his head vigorously.

'Okay, we got a deal.' Nate pulled the buggy to a halt. 'Now why don't you sit in the back and let Mrs Bradford climb up into the comfortable seat? It'll be your first lesson in how to behave like a gentleman.'

* * *

When they reached the orphanage, Sister Alice was waiting for them at the entrance, with a warm smile on her face.

'Bernardo,' she said gently, after they had stepped down from the buggy. 'Go and wash your hands and prepare for supper.'

Bernardo showed visible signs of relief.

‘We do not starve our children here, Bernardo, not even naughty ones. You know that well enough now.’ She turned to Nate and Connie. ‘And you will both stay, yes?’

‘We don’t want to impose,’ said Connie.

‘Of course we’ll stay,’ said Nate firmly. ‘Then I’ll run Mrs Bradford back home.’

‘I could walk . . . ’

‘It’ll be dark in a few hours. I’m not allowing you to walk back alone. Not with Hunter’s men still out there.’

It was easy to forget that the bandits were still out in the hills and might strike at any moment. Ocasa seemed so peaceful.

‘Things happen slowly here,’ said Sister Alice, as if reading Connie’s thoughts. ‘Even the bandits. Which means we never know when they will strike. Come, both of you. Wash up.’

‘Can I help in any way?’ said Connie.

‘You already have,’ said the nun. Connie guessed from her words that the other children had told her about Bernardo's problems.

'I actually came to speak to you about Bernardo,' said Connie.

'So did I, as a matter of fact,' said Nate.

The nun beamed. 'So, you are both in accord,' she said, with a mysterious smile. It was similar to the one that Sofia and the Reverend shared whenever Nate and Connie were mentioned in the same breath. 'We will talk over supper. Come, come . . . The children have been waiting for Bernardo's return and they are very hungry.'

* * *

'You won't punish him too harshly, will you?' asked Connie as they ate supper. It was peasant fare, but filling and very spicy. Connie and Nate were sitting at the top table in the small dining hall, with the nuns.

'He will be made to do some extra chores for a week or two,' said Sister

Alice. 'Nothing too onerous, I promise you. We had one young nun here who tried to make the children rub her smelly feet if they had been naughty. I sent her away very quickly!'

Nate then explained to Sister Alice about the offer he had made Bernardo. 'I hope his punishment won't prevent him from coming up to my ranch as soon as possible.'

'No, that is not going to be a problem. It is a good idea. It will help you too. Although I feel . . . ' Sister Alice paused and became thoughtful for a moment or to. 'Yes, I feel that even in these past few weeks you have begun to find yourself again, Nathan.'

'I haven't been called that in a long time.'

'Nathan? Is that your real name?' asked Connie.

'Yep. But Melissa couldn't say it, so it got shortened to Nate.'

Connie felt as though a cloud passed over the table.

Sister Alice genuflected. 'She would

want you to live life, Nathan,' said the kindly nun. 'Not locked away, as you have been in that mausoleum.'

'My house is not a mausoleum.'

'It is not far from it,' said Sister Alice vehemently. 'Still, I gather it has become a bit more of a home recently. With that young woman and her baby staying.' There was something disapproving in the nun's tone. It surprised Connie as Sister Alice was usually non-judgmental.

'Actually, Mrs Bradford,' said Nate, 'I wanted to talk to you about Cindy-Lou.'

'Oh.' Connie tried to smile brightly, but felt her smile stretch across her face as her heart became constricted.

'Yeah, she hitched her wagon to the wrong star and won't be told. I was kind of hoping that you could talk to her.'

'Hitched her wagon to a what?' Connie frowned, unused to the idiom.

'Got involved with the wrong guy,' said Nate. 'Little Artie's father. Turns out he's in Hunter's gang. She's intent on going to find him as soon as she recovers from her injuries, convinced that he'd never have blown up the train if he'd known she was on it. I'm not so sure about that.

'My housekeeper, Maria, has tried talking to her — she's kind of adopted Cindy-Lou and the baby, which is why they're still up at my place.' Nate spoke firmly and glared at Sister Alice, who just smiled benignly and dipped crackers into her chilli. 'But she won't listen. I figured, with you being younger, Mrs Bradford, you might be able to make her see sense.'

'I'm not sure what I could say. I don't have much experience of men.'

'But you were married,' said Sister Alice, mildly.

Connie felt she was being reminded of the fact, but could not understand why.

'Yes . . . of course . . . What I mean is that George was a kind, reliable man. So I haven't really had problems with men . . . as such.'

'Didn't you tell Senora Youlgreave you were jilted?' Nate's eyes challenged her. Why did she get the feeling he was trying to trip her up?

'Nathan!' Sister Alice reached out and slapped his hand, which made Connie want to laugh. 'That is a very ill-mannered thing to ask a lady. What woman would want to be reminded of the time a man left her at the altar? For that, you can help Bernardo wash the dishes.'

'Yes, Sister Alice.'

Connie did laugh then. He sounded like a recalcitrant ten-year-old.

'I'll dry them,' she offered, wanting to show solidarity.

'No, no, you will go and sit on the sand, Mrs Bradford,' said Sister Alice. 'It is good for men to wash dishes once in a while. It helps to teach them they don't rule us.'

'I never thought we did,' said Nate with a smile. 'If being brought up here taught me anything, it was that.'

* * *

Connie sat on a large rock and relaxed as the sea breeze cooled her face. Glancing up, she saw the Melissa Ranch high on the cliff above her. It looked imposing and magnificent. She could see Cindy-Lou walking along the cliff top, her baby in her arms. Connie waved, but Cindy-Lou was not looking in her direction.

After a few moments, further along the cliff and away from the ranch, the young mother was joined by a tall, thin man. Connie guessed he was one of Nate's ranch hands, though he looked a little unkempt. Whilst Nate's men had well-worn working clothes, sometimes covered in the dust of the day, they were clean. Even from a distance, the man looked scruffy and unclean.

Cindy-Lou and the man seemed to be arguing. The man stormed off. Cindy-Lou stood watching him for a while, and then meekly followed him. They disappeared, somewhere beyond

Connie's line of sight.

'I used to sit there, gazing up at that ranch and promising myself I'd own it one day,' said Nate, sitting down next to her. 'I promised Melissa we'd live there, and she'd have all the pretty dresses she wanted. She used to say it didn't matter what we had, as long as we were together. But I wanted to give her a better life than the one my pa had given us.'

Connie turned her head to listen, but said nothing.

'We lived in New York for a time, while I went to Law School. I worked in a restaurant at night, waiting tables. So we struggled even then, but we managed to eat. After then, I spent a couple of years working as a lawyer. Then I heard old man Rogers, who owned the ranch, had died and his family were looking to sell it on. I had enough money saved, so I bought it and we headed home. My idea was to work as a lawyer here.'

'So what happened?' Connie whispered, after a silence.

'Our stagecoach was ambushed by bandits. Men like Hunter's men. They knocked me and the driver out. Tied up the other passengers.'

He was silent for a long time, as if the memory were too painful.

'When I woke up, Melissa was gone. We found her three days later, after I followed their trail. I should have stopped them taking her.'

'How could you, if they had knocked you out?'

'I was supposed to take care of her. And I didn't. So they took her and . . . they . . . they killed her. That's about all you need to know.'

There was much left unspoken, and whilst Connie was fairly innocent, she understood tacitly that poor Melissa had suffered badly at the hands of the bandits.

'Did you ever find the men who murdered her?' she ventured.

He turned away abruptly. 'It's time I took you home.'

* * *

Nate said nothing else until they were heading back towards Ocasa. The sun was setting behind them and in the peaceful evening, with just the sound of the wheels and the clip of hooves on the rough ground, it was easy to believe they were the only two people in the world.

Connie was acutely aware of the masculine presence of the man sitting next to her. She also sensed a danger in his stillness, like a volcano waiting to erupt. He was a man overwhelmed by pain, and she had to fight the impulse to reach up and stroke his cheek.

'I trailed them with a posse.' He spoke so suddenly, it made her jump. 'Found them about six months later. I did the right thing then. I took them to the sheriff, and they went to trial.

'The leader had a hot-shot lawyer. The type of lawyer I was intending to be. The case was dismissed on a technicality.'

Nate reached up and rubbed the scar on his face.

'Did he give you the scar? The leader of the bandits? Was it when they knocked you out?'

Even as she asked, Connie knew that was not the answer.

'Not then, no. I lost all faith in the law. How could a man like that do what he did to an innocent girl and just walk free? That wasn't why I studied law. So I trailed him again. It took me two years. I found him in a bar in Texas. He didn't even know who I was. Can you believe that? He'd met me on the day they took Melissa, then seen me again in court, but he couldn't even remember my face. I guess he'd hurt so many people during his criminal activities, he just blocked their faces out.

'When I stood next to him at the bar, I saw him appraising me. Two years on the road, sometimes having to fight my way out of trouble, had roughened some of my edges. I wasn't a college boy any more. He thought I was the sort of man he could respect, maybe even do business with. I took his drink, then threw it in his face. I stood in the bar, and told everyone what this man had done to my sister and that I'd come to kill him. Do you know what he did?'

'No . . . ' Connie found she was holding her breath.

'He laughed at me. He remembered me then. Remembered what a tender-foot I'd been when he'd ambushed the stagecoach. Then he laughed about Melissa . . . I stood there with my gun in my hand, ready to shoot him. In cold blood if necessary. I told him I was going to shoot him, but I couldn't do it. All that time, hunting him down and I couldn't kill him.

'All my resolve, all my courage, left me, and all I had was my belief that it was wrong to take another man's life — no matter how bad a man he was. Because that's how I felt when the sheriff shot my father, twenty-five years ago. He didn't *have* to shoot him. They made an example of my pa — just as

Yes, I uttered those very words. But if you don't mind, I had some business to complete with young Mrs Bradford here, so if you could call and see me another day . . .'

'No, it can't wait. There was a problem with the payroll last week.'

From what Sofia had told Connie, Mr Fletcher handled the local payrolls for many of the businesses in the town.

Mr Fletcher drew himself up to his full height. 'I do assure you, Mr Truman, that I always work most diligently on your accounts, Sir.'

'I'm not suggesting otherwise, Mr Fletcher. I'm sure it's just a misunderstanding. But I really need to sort it out — and as I'm here now, I'd like to get it over with. I'm sure Mrs Bradford won't mind me jumping the queue.'

'No, not at all,' said Connie, relief sweeping over her. 'I have all the money I need at the moment, so there's no rush. I insist you sort out Mr Truman's problem first, Mr Fletcher.'

'Then we're decided,' said Nate. He

tipped his hat to Connie. 'Thank you, Ma'am, for your generosity.

'You're welcome. I'll leave you two gentlemen to it.'

Connie walked on, not really relishing facing Sofia. She could see her standing at the doorway as she approached home, an excited expression on her face.

But before Connie could open the garden gate, she noticed a small figure in the distance. Bernardo was sitting on the milestone which marked out the coast road, crying his heart out.

9

'Bernardo, dear, what's wrong?' Connie rushed up the road to him, closely followed by Sofia.

'Mr Estevez said I was a bad influence on Billy and that Billy would never have thought of stealing from Senor Tom if not for me. He said that if I come to town again, he is going to spank me. He said he is going to tell Sister Alice to throw me onto the street. So I cannot go back to the orphanage. He said lots of things that I cannot remember now.'

Whatever it was, Billy's father had certainly terrified Bernardo.

'Oh, my brother Paolo is a fool,' said Sofia, waving her arms expressively. 'Do not worry, bambino, I will speak to him. He will not harm you. He is not a bad man, but he is stupid where Billy is concerned. So is his wife. Though God bless them both, I wish them no harm.' Sofia genuflected.

'And,' said Connie, 'I'm certain Sister Alice wouldn't put you out on the street, Bernardo. You must go back, dear. Sister Alice and the other nuns love you.'

'I am afraid to tell her what I have done.'

'I'll come with you and explain,' said Connie.

'I will take you,' said Sofia.

'No, it's all right, Sofia, you go and rest.' Her friend seemed to have doubled in size since the week before. Connie was certain that the Youlgreave baby was getting ready to make an appearance. 'Bernardo and I will walk together, and have a talk.'

'Querida, it is nearly three miles away. In this heat, you will be roasted like a Thanksgiving turkey.'

'The children have to make the journey every day,' returned Connie. 'Twice a day.' There had been discussion in the town committee to provide the children more like a schoolmarm than ever, with those big innocent eyes staring up at me. I tracked down a man determined to kill him, and got him killed in the process. As the story passed along, people thought I had killed him.'

He laughed humourlessly. 'I saw the story in Billy's comic. It is so far off the mark as to be ridiculous. You should despise me for what I did.'

'And you've punished yourself for it ever since.' Connie spoke with quiet intensity. 'I don't know whether what you did was right or wrong. I don't really understand this land very well, only that things are done differently here compared to in England. But I do know you're a good man, and that what you did you did because you were hurt. You lost your sister, the only person you had in the world, and wanted to strike out at the people who hurt her.

'But in the end you did the right thing. You didn't kill him. If someone else did, it wasn't your fault. It was his — because of the life he led.'

Nate shook his head. 'The law is supposed to deal with men like him. It's like I said to the Reverend, we can't have it both ways in this land. We can't be civilised, then rely on the gun if things don't go the way we want. But that's just what I did.

'And now . . . now the townspeople are looking to me to be that kind of man, without knowing that I'm not capable of it. I don't want to be that man, and I won't be forced into it. I want . . . '

'What do you want, Nate?' Forgetting herself for a moment, Connie reached up and touched the scar on his face.

He turned his burning eyes to look at her, and brought the horse to a halt at the side of the road. And before Connie had a chance to protest — not that she would have wanted to — he had pulled her into his arms, kissing her passionately.

10

Connie lost herself in his embrace, wanting the kiss to last forever; for them to be frozen in that moment, with the sun setting behind them and his arms surrounding her. If she needed any proof that she was in love with him, the kiss confirmed what her heart had been saying for days. As his hungry mouth explored hers, she stroked the nape of his neck tentatively.

When Nate reluctantly pulled back and looked down at her face in the fading light, she could see a faint gleam in his eye. His mouth curved into a deliciously lazy smile.

'I think that I'm not the only one with secrets,' he whispered.

'What do you mean?' Connie's eyes widened and she moved away a little. Had she been wrong to let him kiss her? Perhaps it gave him the impression that she let men kiss her all the time, when in reality it was the first kiss she had ever known. She had never been in this situation, and did not know how to respond. Her parents had sheltered her, and when they died, Elizabeth had continued to do so, determined to make sure Connie would not be hurt as she had been. But perhaps, thought Connie, she had been too sheltered. It left her adrift in a world of men she did not quite understand. Her only experience of men was her late brother-in-law and she was acutely aware that Nate was nothing like George. She wondered if George had the same effect on Elizabeth as Nate had on her, but could not even begin to imagine it.

He turned sharply away and lightly pulled at the reins so that the horse started walking again. 'So — this is how it's going to be, is it? I tell you everything about myself, but you still don't trust me enough to tell me the truth about you.'

'If you think that I'm easy . . . '

To her surprise and consternation he laughed. 'No — that's not at all what I was thinking.'

'What were you thinking?'

'I was thinking that if we're going to work, then you have to learn to trust me. Trust that I'll never let you down, no matter what happens.'

'Are you talking about the situation Cindy-Lou is in? With . . . with the baby?' The heat rose in Connie's face. 'Because if you are, I can assure you that won't happen just because you kissed me. I've no intention of hitching my wagon to any wrong stars.'

The full sensuous lips that had kissed her became a thin line on his face. 'Well, at least we got that clear. Seems to me you and Old Tom feel the same way about bad blood.'

'No, no, I didn't mean that.' Tears pricked her eyes. He had completely misunderstood her. 'I simply meant that I'm not going to get myself into trouble like Cindy did. I didn't mean about you . . . '

'Don't worry about it. When you're old, you'll be able to tell your grandkids about the time a bad man, just like Jesse James, kissed you.'

'You're not a bad man. I don't believe that for one minute!' How had things turned sour so soon? 'I wish . . . I wish time could turn back to when you kissed me. Then I might be able to say and do the things you wanted me to say and do. I'm sorry I got it so wrong.'

He did not answer. They reached the outskirts of Ocasa, and Nate gee'd the horse up until he pulled the buggy to a shuddering halt outside the Youlgreaves' home. Despite his anger, he got down off the buggy and walked around to her side to help her down.

'Please, Nate . . . Let's not leave things like this.' His strong hands on her waist, burning through the fabric of her dress, were almost more than she could bear. For a moment she thought he might kiss her again. She wished he would. It might put things right.

But he stepped back and tipped his hat. 'Goodnight . . . Mrs Bradford.'

* * *

Connie stirred the pot of stew above the fire, wiped her hands and stood back to admire her handiwork. For the first time, she would be spending the night in a home that was all hers.

The cottage was exactly as she wanted it. A fire burned in the grate, to keep out the cold of the evening. Pretty curtains, courtesy of Sofia, hung at the windows in the main room and the bedroom. She had acquired a rocking chair, a table and some other pieces of furniture from the townspeople, who despite her protestations had insisted on helping her to furnish the cottage.

Sofia had also given her a thick quilt for the bed, made from a myriad of different fabrics and colours. It was the prettiest thing Connie had ever seen, and she had a vague notion of making one of her own, for when the current bedspread needed to be washed. It would be something to do in the long evenings in her perfect little home. True, the privy was out back, but she supposed one could not have everything.

She walked across to the front door, which she had recently painted. With a smile of satisfaction, and being careful not to touch the still wet paint, she closed it and drew the bolt across.

Sofia had begged her to wait. 'Querida, there is no rush to leave us. Wait a few days. I do not see why you want to live alone in that cottage, anyway. You are with family here. We love you and take care of you.'

For days, since Nate had dropped Connie off the evening they kissed, Sofia had been hungry for information. The reverend's fiery wife knew something had happened, probably due to Connie's stricken appearance when she had walked into the house, but Connie had resisted all attempts by Sofia to gain information. She would not tell

Nate's secret, but neither could she bring herself to tell the truth about the kiss. Sofia would no doubt rush off to the Melissa Ranch and demand Nate married Connie. It was her friend's loving but overwhelming way.

If truth be known, Connie found Sofia's need to care for her a little cloying. And there was another reason. If Nate's kiss had taught her anything, it was that she had spent far too much of her life under the care of others, and it had not equipped her adequately in how to deal with the world. With men in particular. It would be easy to give herself up to Sofia's care, but it would also be dangerous. There was something comforting about letting someone else do all your thinking for you, and Connie needed the time and experience to think for herself.

She put a pot of coffee on the fire and sat down in her rocking chair, letting its movement soothe her. Idly, and with a faint smile on her lips, she imagined herself being called Old

Connie at some time in the distant future, like Old Tom at the store.

That was when she remembered that she was not Connie Ruddick any more. She was Elizabeth Bradford. And if she stayed here in Ocasa, she would have to keep that name for the rest of her life.

Unless she married.

That thought brought the motion of the chair to a halt. That would never happen. *Could* never happen. She was not entirely sure of the law on the matter, but if she married as Elizabeth Bradford, she feared it would almost certainly not be legal.

The simple life she had imagined for herself in the cottage suddenly became complicated again. But, she thought, as she resumed rocking the chair, it was not complicated. Because she would simply never marry. She loved Nate with her heart and soul, and could not imagine feeling that way about any other man.

He had not spoken to her since that night, only tipping his hat politely if they happened to meet in the town. But she noticed he had stopped coming down, and started sending his men again. Earlier that day, she had seen him dropping Cindy-Lou and baby Artie off in the town, before he rode off somewhere else. From Cindy-Lou's expression it was clear that she admired Nate. How could she not? He was a handsome man. And, Connie had to concede, remembering how he had been with Bernardo, he would make a much better father figure for little Artie. He had treated Bernardo with just the right balance of sternness and compassion. Her father would have liked him very much.

She felt tears prick her eyes, and impatiently brushed them away. She had not meant to cry. She was supposed to feel happy on the first night in her new home. But sitting in the silence, with not even Sofia to talk to any more and with Nate heavily on her mind, she felt isolated.

Perhaps, she thought, she would walk

down to the Youlgreave's and invite them for supper. It was not a long walk and the sun had not yet set. It might be dark by the time she got there, but then she would have their company coming back. She took a deep breath. No, she would not do that. She would learn to stand on her own two feet.

Connie reached over to stir her stew. As she did so, she heard a branch snap, followed by what sounded like a man's voice cursing.

The cottage was in a clearing on the hillside, but had trees all around it where anyone might hide. She peered through the curtain. It was too dim outside to see anything clearly, but she felt a presence there.

Should she go outside and challenge whoever it was? Or should she stay safely locked behind her door? What if the person broke in?

The idea of living alone lost its glow. It had been a stupid idea to come here. Hunter's men had been quiet since the train derailment, but that did not mean they were not waiting to strike again.

She remembered the warning triangle that Joshua Stephenson had fixed for her. But it was on the porch, above the door, which meant she would have to open the door to reach it. What a stupid idea that had been, too! Why had no one thought of that? She had no gun, and would not even know how to shoot one if she had.

'What a fool you are, Connie,' she whispered, as fear gripped her. Nate had been vague about what happened to Melissa, to protect her. But her imagination was enough to convince her that it might just happen to her tonight. And all because she had insisted on being alone. She longed for Sofia's warm and rapid chatter to fill up the evening, or the Reverend's more thoughtful conversation. How ungrateful she had been to the warm-hearted Spaniard and her husband!

When she heard another sound, she screamed involuntarily.

'Who is it?' she called through the

door. 'Go away. I'm armed. I've got a rifle and I will shoot you.'

She heard soft laughter, recognising the voice immediately.

'Open the door. It's me.'

With trembling fingers, she did as she was bid.

'This was why I decided to keep watch tonight,' said Nate, as he stood on the porch, so tall that his head nearly hit the warning triangle. 'Never tell a man you've got a gun when you haven't. And never, ever open the door just because you think you hear someone you can trust.'

He looked at her for a long time, so that she thought her heart would stop. 'But I guess I know now that you do trust me.'

11

'You're not holding it properly. Squeeze it gently.' Nate adjusted the rifle in Connie's hands. It was hard to explain to him that the fact of him standing so close behind her, encircling her in his arms, was very distracting. He had not kissed her since that first time, even though she'd longed for him to. But they had become friends again, the awkwardness between them evaporating as they had shared the stew in her cottage several nights before. She supposed she would have to settle for that.

'It nearly broke my shoulder, Nate.'

'Yeah, you'll get a little recoil. Now, hold it steady, looking down the sight, and point at the cans on the fence.'

They were at the Melissa Ranch, where Nate had insisted she go to learn how to shoot. Several yards away, lined up along the fence, were a row of tin cans. Connie could have done without the spectators — in this case, Nate's ranch hands and Bernardo — all of whom found the scenario highly amusing.

'I thought that English gentlemen were into hunting, shooting and fishing,' Nate said. She could feel his warm breath on her ear, and had to comfort herself with the fact that, were she ever in a situation where she needed to shoot to defend herself, he would not be there disturbing her equilibrium in this way.

'English gentlemen, yes. I'm a woman.'

'I had noticed.' She was glad he said it quietly, so the others could not hear. She did fear they could see her blushes. 'Now squeeze the trigger slowly, like I showed you.'

Connie tried to shut him out of her mind, and pretend that she could not feel him pressed against her back. Only as she pulled the trigger, she inadvertently moved back a little, so that they were closer than ever. The shot went wide, lodging in a tree trunk yards away from the cans.

'Well,' he laughed, 'at least you hit something that time. Fellas, I think you all better stand back a bit.'

The men shuffled back a few feet, chuckling amongst themselves. Bernardo laughed the loudest.

'I'm not going to do it if you're going to make fun of me.' She pouted.

'Then I'll move all your stuff over and you can live here until I'm sure you can take care of yourself.'

Connie fought the impulse to beg him to do just that. 'I can take care of myself. Besides, you've got enough people to take care of, with Cindy-Lou and baby Artie.' The words came out sounding more brittle than Connie intended.

'So that's what's been bugging you.' He exhaled slowly. 'There is nothing between me and Cindy-Lou. I gave a girl a home with her baby because . . . well, because I actually thought it was what you wanted, after you risked your life to save little Artie. Surely you wouldn't want me to put the child out on the streets, would you now?'

'Of course not.' It was in her mind to point out there were plenty of other places in Ocasa where they could stay, but it would sound churlish.

'And she couldn't have stayed anywhere else, because some of the good folks of Ocasa have strong ideas about unmarried mothers.' He had a truly annoying habit of reading her mind. 'They might greet them in the street, to be neighbourly, but they're not going to let them into their homes. Except maybe Senora Youlgreave — and you were staying there. I figured that with the Senora's baby due any time soon, she had enough people to care for. I guess I could have sent her down to the orphanage, but Sister Alice told me only recently that they're full up at the moment.'

'Oh.' Connie was lost for words.

That Cindy-Lou might be made unwelcome in Ocasa had never occurred to her, perhaps because the townspeople had been so welcoming to her and seemed so kind to everyone else. Then she remembered what Old Tom had said about the orphans, and the Estevezes' insistence that Bernardo was to blame for what happened that day, not Billy. She also remembered how dismissive one of the women from the town had been about baby Artie on the night of the train derailment. Had that been because the woman had seen that Cindy-Lou was not wearing a wedding ring?

That there was a less welcoming undercurrent in the town bothered Connie. It did not bode well if her own secret were ever discovered.

'Hey?' Nate lightly touched her earlobe, sending a shiver of delight coursing through her.

'What is it?'

'Nothing — I was just bringing you back from wherever it was you drifted off to.'

'I really think I've had enough shooting lessons today, Nate. I ought to be getting home.'

'No, don't go. Stay for lunch and we'll try again later. I'll tell the guys to keep out of the way. I can see they're putting you off.'

It was not the men, but Connie did not want to tell him that. She nodded and smiled. She wanted to spend more time with him.

'Do you mind if Bernardo joins us?' he asked.

'No, of course not,' she said. It might be better if the child was there. She would have to act naturally in front of him. That was harder during moments when she and Nate were alone, or far enough away from others that it felt as if they were alone.

'Senor Truman.' Maria, the housekeeper, was waiting at the door for them. She smiled a warm welcome at Connie before becoming earnest.

'What is it, Maria? Is lunch ready?'

'Si, but . . . it has happened again, Senor Truman.'

Nate gave an exasperated sigh. 'How

much this time?'

'Ten dollars — and some of the silver from the dresser.'

'What's happening?' asked Connie.

'Something I was hoping I wouldn't have to tell you,' said Nate. 'Come on into the dining room. Maria, would you serve lunch, please? And don't worry.' He touched his housekeeper on the arm. 'I'll get your silver back.'

'It is your silver, Senor Truman.'

'Yeah, but you treat it as if it's your own.' He smiled at her.

'I do good work for a good man,' said Maria, as she went back towards the kitchen.

Connie started to follow Nate, only to find that Bernardo remained in the doorway, his eyes wide and frightened.

'What is it, Bernardo?'

'I did not do it, Senora Bradford. I swear I did not take the silver.'

'No, I'm sure no one thinks you did.'

'Bernardo.' Nate turned back. 'No one said you did. Come on in and I'll tell you and Mrs Bradford all about it.'

After a few moments at the lunch table, where Nate poured them fresh orange juice and Maria served them cold meat and potatoes, Bernardo began to relax a little.

'We know you didn't do it, Bernardo,' Nate repeated, when he finished drinking his orange juice. 'We think . . . ' Nate stopped and looked sternly at Bernardo. 'Nothing I say here is to be mentioned in town, Bernardo. Not to Billy or anyone. You know how these things get around. The only reason I'm letting you hear all this is so you know I don't suspect you.'

'I understand. I will not say anything.'

'Good boy. We think it's Cindy-Lou.'

'Cindy-Lou took the silver?' said Connie.

'I'm afraid so. The first time she did it, it was just a few dollars that I'd left on the dresser over there. I know Maria wouldn't take it and the guys seldom come into the house. Anyway, Cindy-Lou admitted it. Said she needed money for some things for baby Artie

and just saw it there and picked it up. I told her that if she needed anything, I'd get it for her. I wouldn't see the child go without warm clothes or diapers. I was also paying her to help Maria. Not much, because most of her time was spent with the baby. Which is as it should be. But then other things went missing. Small items, like a cigar box — or, in one case, a gun. Then some money that Maria had in the kitchen to pay the tradesmen went missing. Now this. I think she's stealing it for someone.'

'I saw her talking to a man on the clifftop,' said Connie. 'I thought it was one of your men, but he seemed too unkempt. I wonder . . . '

'Big Artie?'

Connie nodded thoughtfully. 'Yes, I think it probably was. She was . . . is . . . very attached to him. And it would explain why Hunter's men haven't raided. They've found an easier way to get money.'

'I haven't seen him around. Neither

have my men. But if he came up when everyone was about their evening chores we could easily miss him. We're on the lookout for a group of men — Hunter's men — not just one guy.' He squared his shoulders. 'I'll talk to her when she comes back.'

* * *

Cindy-Lou did not return that day, nor the next. Nate called at Connie's cottage on Sunday afternoon. They sat together on the front porch swing, drinking orange juice which Nate had brought with him, courtesy of Maria.

'She just disappeared,' Nate explained. 'Left all her luggage, and most of Baby Artie's things, and took off.'

'You don't think she's living up in the hills with the bandits, do you?'

Nate shrugged. 'Who knows? She can't have taken the train out of here. They're still repairing the tracks. And no one at the coach stop has seen her. She didn't have a horse, so the only way

she could leave was on someone else's horse or on foot.'

'Oh Nate, that poor baby up in the hills. We should go looking for her.'

'We?' He raised an eyebrow. 'Look, I know you're concerned about the baby, but Cindy-Lou is his mama. She made the decision to go up there — if that is where she's gone. She's over the age of majority, we can't go and simply drag her back.'

'I'm worried about her, too. We might be able to make her see sense.'

'And we might get our heads blown off in the process. We could walk straight into a trap. Hunter's men must be getting desperate.'

'I can't understand why she left your ranch. If she was getting money for them by stealing it from you,' said Connie.

'Maybe she realised she'd gone too far.' He looked grim. 'Reached the end of my hospitality.'

'Where would they sell the silver? The nearest town is forty miles off.'

'They could be stockpiling it, for

later. There are some old watering holes scattered around about, where the mine workers used to go and where the stage-coaches sometimes stop to rest their horses. Some places aren't too fussy, given that they have to rely on passing trade.'

'I wish we could do something, Nate. For Cindy-Lou and the baby.'

'You can't save everyone,' he said, gently. 'You certainly can't save some-one from themselves.' He reached across and touched her hair. 'You'll only end up being hurt.'

She felt herself melting at the tender-ness of the gesture, but her anxious thoughts were still on the wayward young mother.

'You'd think with having the baby to care about, Cindy-Lou would have more sense,' she said fretfully.

He sighed. 'I think the same about my pa.'

'Yes — I suppose being a parent doesn't always make one face up to one's responsibilities, as it should.'

'Some parents drag their kids from

one place to the next, from one bad situation to the next.'

Connie swallowed hard and looked at him imploringly.

'But if we could only persuade her to let us take care of Baby Artie, Nate! She could follow Big Artie wherever she wanted to, then.'

He looked astonished at her suggestion. 'You want to take on someone else's child? How are you going to work at the school and care for a child, on your own? And what happens if she shows up some years down the line, wanting him back? What then?'

Connie's spirits drooped. 'I don't know. I just hate to think of another child growing up to have the life of terrible hardship that you did.'

'Like I said, you can't save everyone.'

'No — and I didn't save you.'

'No?' He touched her hair again and her heart quivered. 'I'm not so sure about that.'

'You sorted out your own life long before I arrived here.'

'But you're the first person, apart from Sister Alice, who has accepted me knowing all that. I admit I was afraid before. Of what people would say. Sure, they're talking, now they know about my father — but the reputation I built up over the past five years has stopped them from turning against me. I'm not sure what they'd say if they knew about me tracking down a man . . . '

'But you didn't kill him!'

'After hunting him down for two years with the sole intention of killing him. They might not turn against me straight away. They'd be looking to me to sort out the Hunter problem. No one wants to get their hands dirty, but they don't mind if someone else does it. And if I did, then they'd turn against me. Because as much as they want me to help them, they don't really want men like me living amongst them, walking the same streets as their wives and children. Not in a civilised town.'

'I won't tell anyone. You know that, don't you?'

'I know.' He held her gaze for a long time, as her heart beat faster and she felt a tingle in her spine. 'We need to talk, you and I,' he murmured.

'About what?'

'Lots of things. The truth, for a start . . . '

'Senor Truman . . . Senor Truman!'

Bernardo came running up through the trees, gasping for breath, his hair and clothes unkempt. 'I told him not to go but he would not listen and now Senor Estevez comes to the orphanage and blames me and I ran away and . . . ' Bernardo slumped on his knees in front of Connie's porch.

'Bernardo, calm down,' said Connie, rising from her seat.

Nate got up too. 'Here, drink this.' He handed the boy a glass of orange juice, which he drank down in one gulp, almost choking.

'Take your time and tell us all about it.'

'I ran all the way from the orphanage,' Bernardo gasped. 'To the ranch, but they said you had gone. I knew you would come to see Senora Bradford, so I ran here. I have a stitch in my side.'

'Shh, dear, get your breath back and tell us what's wrong.'

It took Bernardo several minutes to stop gasping long enough to tell them. He kept trying to speak before he was able to breathe calmly again, which slowed down his progress. 'Billy Estevez . . . His mama and papa sent him to bed without supper, because Senora Youlgreave told them the truth about the other day. Then this morning Billy left a note for his mama and papa . . . he said he was going to be a bandit. To live in the hills. They have been looking for him all day, then Senor Estevez was so angry he came to the orphanage, shouting at Sister Alice, saying it was my fault.' Bernardo burst into tears.

Connie stooped down and put her arms around the child.

'Nate . . . ' She looked up at him and saw the muscle in his cheekbone twitch, as if he were trying hard to control his emotions.

'This is not our problem,' he answered.

'Nate. There are two children up in the hills now. You said if we went up there, we'd get our heads blown off. What if they do that to Billy?'

'Don't look at me like that! Like you expect me to be the one to sort this out. Not after what we just talked about here. If Estevez wants his son back, he can damn well go and get him.'

He slapped his leg in a gesture of frustration. 'Damn it, if he knew the kid was going into the hills, why has he wasted all day hanging around here looking for him? I'll tell you why. Because he's too scared. Even to go and save his son.' His eyes flashed with contempt. 'Well, if he can't stand up like a man and care for his own, I don't see why I should.'

Nate stormed off the porch and untied his horse from the rail, throwing himself into the saddle. 'I can't believe you,' he said, his eyes blazing at Connie. 'After all I've told you, I thought you'd understand. You're as bad as the rest of them. I'm sorry I can't be what you expect me to be. I'm not Jesse James.' He turned his horse and galloped off into the trees.

'Nate!' Connie gazed after him, wringing her hands.

12

As they reached the orange grove where Sofia had taken Connie on her first full day in Ocasa, Connie turned to the dishevelled boy beside her and spoke firmly. 'Bernardo, I want you to go back now.'

'I do not want to let you go up there alone, Senora Bradford.'

'I said you could come this far with me, but that's all, Bernardo. Sister Alice would never forgive me if anything happened to you.'

And Connie would never forgive herself either, if Bernardo were hurt, she added silently.

'What if Old Tom is wrong?'

An hour before, they'd stopped at the town so that Connie could ask Old Tom where the old mine workings were. She suspected that if Tom had mentioned it to Billy as a possible hiding place for

Hunter and his men, it would be where Billy headed.

'Old Tom won't be wrong. He's a silly old man sometimes, but he does know the area. Please, dear. Go back now.'

'Senor Truman will be angry with you.'

'Well,' said Connie, trying to sound confident, 'I'm not as afraid of Senor Truman as you are.' Besides, she reasoned, Nate was already angry with her. A little more anger would not make much difference.

'I am not really afraid of him. Though I would be, if I thought he would be angry with me. He might be angry with me if I do not take care of you.'

'Bernardo, dearest, Senor Truman won't expect you to take care of me. You're just a little boy. In fact, he's more likely to be furious with me for letting you come this far.'

'But if you are not afraid of him, it does not matter.'

'You are too clever for your own good, do you know that?' Connie laughed, and it helped release some of the tension she was feeling.

'I don't think Hunter and his men are going to be up there. But I do think it's where Billy has gone. So I don't need you to protect me, though I'm awfully grateful that you want to. Now, go back. Tell Sister Alice where I've gone and why, and perhaps she'll send Billy's father up here.'

'I could go to Senor Estevez's house and tell him.'

'No, because he may still be angry with you.' It seemed to Connie that anger was the order of the day. Nate was angry, Paolo Estevez was angry. The very air seemed to crackle with fury. If she were honest, she would have to admit she was also angry, and disappointed with Nate.

She knew it was unfair, and that protecting the town from the bandits should not just fall to him. But she had made a personal plea to him, for the sake of two children, and he had simply ridden away. It was with a growing sense of shame that she realised the only reason she was going up into the hills was to teach him a lesson for not caring about Billy and Baby Artie.

'Go to Sister Alice and let her deal with it.' On seeing his doubtful expression, Connie added persuasively, 'Someone has to tell people where I've gone, Bernardo. If we both go, then no one can fetch help.'

It was not strictly true. Old Tom knew where they were going — or must have guessed. But Connie did not want to draw Bernardo into any more danger. She had the idea that if she went into the hills alone, she would be less conspicuous than a posse. If the bandits were there, she might be able to draw Billy away from them. She might be able to enlist Cindy-Lou's help. She had to hope the girl had some conscience.

'Go back, Bernardo. Please. I'll have enough to worry about, bringing Billy back. I can't be responsible for both of you.' She saw that she had hurt his feelings, so put her arms around him and hugged him to her. 'I know you're a brave, clever boy, but I really don't want anything to happen to you.'

'I do not want anything to happen to you,' the boy returned.

'It won't. I'll probably be much safer than if we went up there with a posse of men, Bernardo. They'll just think I'm a silly woman who got lost. At least; that's what I'm hoping will happen. Now please — go back to Sister Alice.'

Bernardo walked away reluctantly, taking a last look back at her. 'I shan't move until I see you near to the edge of town,' she said. 'So you needn't think you're going to wait and then follow me. Now, run! It will be getting dark in an hour or two.'

Bernardo took a few half-hearted steps, then began to run. Connie sensed he was crying and hated herself for putting him in an impossible situation. She should never have let him accompany her so far.

She waited until he reached the town, where he stopped and waved, looking smaller than ever in the distance. Connie turned and ducked amongst the trees, deliberately ensuring he lost sight of her, so that he would not try to follow.

Once she passed the cultivated orange groves, the hillside became craggier, with a few trees giving cover. Even these petered out towards the top of the hill, turning into a rocky, uneven terrain. She could see a ledge above her, and the dark shadows that signified the openings of the old mine workings. She could imagine Billy would have no trouble getting up there, but wondered how Cindy-Lou managed it with a baby in her arms. If, indeed, they were up there. Connie was exhausted and she only had herself to carry up the hill. Her dress clung to her back, beads of perspiration prickling down her spine.

As she grew nearer to the ledge, the light began to grow dimmer, and the air turned its usual shade of pink as the

sun set behind her. N
stop and look. Every
they had seen the sun
times. But she had to kee

A fire burned somewh
guessed that it must be ab
she was too far from the tow
the smoke from the homestea
She idly wondered if Billy had m
He might have taken them from h

She stopped to rest against a
trying to keep out of sight of the led
In a few more yards, she would be clea
of the trees completely, with nothing
but a few large rocks for cover. At some
point, she would have no choice but to
step out into the open. It was getting
darker still, as the sun set lower in the
east. She had not brought a lantern, as
she had not wanted to carry too much.
So if she found Billy, she would have to
find her way back with him in the dark.

'You're so stupid,' she whispered to
herself. Now she was near the top of
the hill, her resolve began to fail. She
should have told Billy's father about the

Despite Nate's harsh words, it ossible that Paolo Estevez had not ght of Billy going up into the hills. might not have believed Billy was ng to the bandits, given his rose-oured view of his son's behaviour. e probably thought the child was ding at a friend's or somewhere else n the vicinity of the town.

And perhaps, thought Connie with a heavy heart, that was exactly where Billy was. Given how she felt, having reached this point, she wondered if a child's enthusiasm for going up into the hills would wane even sooner. Especially if he became hungry and thirsty. She cursed herself for not picking some oranges on her way up. Her only thought had been to reach the top of the hill and find Billy. And . . . teach Nate a lesson.

That thought shamed her again. It was wrong of her to put so much pressure on him, especially after all he had told her. She had let him down. Now, with only a few trees between

herself and exposure, what he said about them getting their heads blown off came back to her. If she stepped out of the trees, that was exactly what would happen, if the bandits had a lookout — and she had no doubt they would.

Her blood ran cold. What had happened to Billy when he stepped out of the trees? What if they shot him, and he was lying somewhere amongst the rocks? And what if she had talked Nate into coming up here? Then he would be dead, too.

More than at any time during her few weeks in Ocasa, she longed for the quiet village where she had grown up. She and Elizabeth had been able to walk for hours as children. True, there were places they were warned to keep away from, like an abandoned quarry and a part of the woods where the gamekeeper put traps. But no one ever had to worry about bandits.

In the enormous country to which she had moved, the wide open spaces were deceptive. Far from being safe, they were places were a traveller was at their most vulnerable.

Still holding her back against the tree, Connie turned her upper body and attempted to peer up to the ledge. There was enough light for her to see a thin stream of smoke trailing out from one of the caves further along the ledge. Had Billy lit a fire? Or was it Hunter and his men?

There was only one way she was going to find out. She stepped out from behind the tree and walked a few steps. Then she felt a painful thud on the back of her head and she blacked out.

* * *

'Mrs Bradford? Are you okay?' Billy spoke in a terrified whisper.

Connie opened her eyes, as a searing pain rushed through her head. 'Oh . . . ' she murmured, rubbing her eyes with her hand. They immediately started stinging from the dense smoke that filled the cave.

'Billy . . . Are you hurt?'

'No, Mrs Bradford, but they won't let me go home.' Billy sobbed a little. 'I'm so sorry, Mrs Bradford, I thought they'd be fun, but they ain't. I want to go home to Mama and Papa.'

'We'll get you home, dear, don't worry.' Connie tried to sit up. Whoever had knocked her out had thrown her unceremoniously onto the floor of the cave. Every bone in her body ached from the cold, dank ground. She could just about make out the contours of the cave, by the flickering light of the fire, but the smoke hung in the air, precluding too much illumination. Billy sat up against the opposite side of the cave, his knees pulled up to his chest, and his face dirty and tear-stained.

'How long have I been unconscious, Billy?'

'I don't know. Fifteen minutes, maybe. Mr Hunter put you there. They watched you walk all the way up the hill, and he came out to get you.'

'Where are they now?'

'On the ledge talking about what they'll do with you. They said I wasn't to move and you're not to either, or they'll shoot us.' Billy started to sob.

'Hush now, dear,' said Connie, crawling across and placing her arm around his shoulder. There wasn't much room to stand up in this part of the cave. Nearer to the entrance, the ceiling was nearly tall enough for a man to stand. But that was also where Hunter and his men were. Once Connie had changed position, she could see their dark shadows moving around, and hear them murmuring amongst themselves.

'How much is she worth to Truman, do you think?' One of the men spoke more loudly. His voice was deep and resonant, and Connie guessed it was Hunter. He spoke like a leader.

'I don't know. Why don't you just let her go?'

It was a woman's voice. 'Cindy-Lou,' Connie whispered.

'Yeah, she's here with her baby,' said

Billy. 'They got angry when he cried, so she took him to a different cave.'

'Which one, Billy? Do you know?' Connie started thinking hard about how they were going to escape. Their path was blocked at the moment, but Hunter and his men would have to sleep sometime. Her idea was to find Baby Artie and take him down to Ocasa with Billy. She thought it would probably be considered abduction, but it was preferable to the poor child being with men who grew angry when he cried.

'I don't know. Further along the ledge.'

'Upwards, you mean?'

That would mean having to go further along the ledge, and then back down. She doubted it could be done, and considered that she might just have to leave with Billy. The fact that they had been holding Billy against his will did at least give a reason for the sheriff to come up with a posse. If they could get him sober long enough to arrange it. Connie had only met him properly once, in church — and even then, after they were introduced, he had slumped in the pew, sleeping off a night at the saloon.

Why the townspeople had let the sheriff get away with it so long, she did not know. Perhaps they had been too comfortable until Hunter came along; a quiet little town where everyone knew everyone else, all the families, whether European or Hispanic, joined by marriage, forgiving each others' worst excesses as long as nothing too bad happened. They indulged the sheriff much as the Estevezes indulged Billy. Like a mischievous child who they believed could do no real wrong.

And when the sheriff could not help them, they looked to Nate. Not just because of his reputation, but because he had an authority about him that the others lacked. She remembered the way he had immediately taken command of the meeting from Joshua Stephenson on the day she arrived in town.

Everyone had stopped talking and looked to him.

Billy's grandfather might be the one who did all the talking at the weekly town meetings, but he never actually decided anything or helped others make a decision about the best way to proceed. Whether it was the best way to deal with Hunter's men or laying proper roads through Ocasa, under Joshua's leadership no action was ever really taken.

Not that any of her musing helped her out of the situation she was in. She would not even be able to rouse the sheriff into doing anything, unless she could get Billy back down to the town. She tried not to doubt that she could persuade them.

And if they did bring a posse? What then? Hunter had seen her coming and dealt with her. He may not be able to knock out every member of a posse, but he and his men could pick them off with guns as they moved out of the clearing. Her already aching head spun.

Who was she to judge the townspeople for not acting against Hunter sooner? Everything that had happened, that was happening to her at that moment, was beyond her range of experience.

'We need to get out of here,' she said to Billy.

'I wouldn't try that if I were you.' The man with the deep voice had come into the cave whilst she was lost in her reverie. Connie turned her head to look at the man that held the town to ransom and found herself deeply disappointed. The voice did not match the man. Far from being a tall, dark mysterious man, Hunter — if it was indeed Hunter — was short and stocky with a beer gut. His beard was matted with old food, and his skin greasy. She could smell him from where she sat, though the cave had its own nasty aroma too.

In a way, it proved to her that she was not really much better than Billy when it came to imagining bandits. She had expected Hunter to be more dashing and attractive. *Like Nate,* a little voice said.

Like the men in Billy's comics, another voice said.

The publishers, she decided, had a lot to answer for in the way they glamorised outlaws, because even though Connie thought she was relatively sensible, she now realised that she too had been influenced by the stories and accompanying pictures.

'Mr Hunter?'

He bowed his head in a mock show of courtesy. 'The one and only, ma'am. Frank Hunter, knight of the road.'

Connie fought the impulse to laugh. She had certainly imagined knights to be taller and better-looking.

'And you're Mrs Bradford. The schoolmistress. I been watching you around town for a while.' He licked his lips in a way that Connie found stomach-churning. 'We got a pretty good view of Ocasa from up here.'

'So I hear.'

'I been asking Cindy-Lou how much

you're worth to Mr Truman. Word has it he's sweet on you.'

'Then the word is wrong,' said Connie, sticking her chin out with all the pride she could muster. 'Mr Truman and I are not close.'

She believed at that moment that she spoke the truth. Nate was angry with her, and probably did not care what happened to her. The thought tested her resolve a little, but she was not going to be intimidated by a man who was not much taller than she was.

'Really? That's not what Cindy-Lou says.'

'Cindy-Lou barely knows either of us, Mr Hunter. She's been in Ocasa less time than I have.'

'So he won't care if I kill you?'

Billy started to whimper again.

13

'Please let Billy go home,' begged Connie. 'He's only a child, and he needs his mother.'

'Nope, he's seen too much. He's staying here till I can work out what to do about him.'

It gave Connie some hope that Hunter had no apparent plans to kill Billy. If he had, she was sure Billy would already be dead. Whatever Hunter was, there was a good chance he was not a child killer.

'And if you're thinking I won't kill him if I have to, you're wrong, Mrs Bradford. I don't need no kids slowing me down. I told Artie the same thing when his girl arrived here with that squalling brat. Cindy-Lou!'

Hunter's sudden change of volume made Connie jump. He went to the entrance of the cave. 'Get up here now.

You're supposed to be working for a living. Bring one of the sacks. Mrs Bradford here can help you.'

Cindy-Lou looked at the ground sheepishly when she entered the cave dragging a sack full of mail that was almost as big as she was.

'Hello, Cindy-Lou,' said Connie evenly.

'Hello, Mrs Bradford. You okay?'

It seemed a ridiculous question to ask under the circumstances.

'Not really,' answered Connie tartly.

'Help her sort this mail,' said Hunter. 'Take out any money you find.'

'I will not help you to steal money from the mail!'

'Oh, yes, you will, Mrs Bradford. Look at it this way. While you're useful, I'll let the kid live. How's that for a deal?'

Billy huddled in close to Connie. Hunter left the cave, and Cindy-Lou moved towards the back, putting the sack up against the back wall.

'You better do what he says,' she told

Connie in a flat, downtrodden voice. 'They're not finding enough money — and they were that eager at first that any money they did find was torn when they ripped the envelope open, so they couldn't use it. So the mail's just been sitting there for over a week until I came along and they set me to opening it.'

'How many sacks are there?' asked Connie, trying to work out how long they had.

'There's another six after this one here. They opened most of them.'

'I don't understand. Why would the mail train carry so much when it was near to its final stop?'

'It drops off the incoming mail and picks up the outgoing mail, of course.' Cindy-Lou spoke in a similar tone to the one Connie sometimes used to the slower children. 'The mail that has to go back East, that is. Not the local mail. A different train handles that.'

'I hadn't thought of that,' Connie said, defensively.

'You better get on with it,' said Cindy-Lou.

'I'm in no hurry to be shot, Cindy-Lou.'

'If he sees you not working, you'll be shot anyway. I'm only alive because Big Artie stuck up for me. Here.' Cindy-Lou handed over a few of the letters.

'Why on earth did you come up here?' asked Connie. She held the letters in her hand, reluctant to tamper with someone else's private correspondence.

'To be with Big Artie.'

'And what about Baby Artie? This is no place for him. Where is he?'

'He's in the top cave. It's okay,' Cindy-Lou said hastily when she saw Connie's expression. 'He's not alone, Big Artie is with him. He's such a good daddy to my boy.'

It was on Connie's lips to say that a good father would not let his baby son sleep in a dirty, damp cave, but she suppressed the retort. She needed Cindy-Lou's help — and alienating her by being judgemental about the man the young woman loved would not achieve that.

'You have to help us get away, Cindy-Lou.'

'I can't. Will you open the letters? If he comes back and finds us talking . . . ' The girl put her hand up to her face, and for the first time Connie realised that what she had taken for a shadow on Cindy-Lou's cheek was a newly-formed bruise.

'Big Artie let Hunter do that to you?'

'He didn't let him. It just happened when I argued with them about you. I tried to keep you alive by saying Mr Truman would pay ransom money to get you back, then you go and tell Hunter that's not so.'

'Oh . . . Well, thank you for that, anyway. But they would soon realise the money would not materialise.'

'I'm not so sure. Mr Truman likes you a lot.'

'Not at the moment, he doesn't.' Connie heard someone near the entrance of the cave, and saw Hunter's legs come into view. Afraid he might come in and hurt her or Billy, she turned one of the letters over and made as if to open it. The form outside the cave moved on.

'You got to do it, Mrs Bradford. Open the mail like he said.' Cindy-Lou's voice held a pleading note. 'Please. If he thinks I've failed . . . '

'It's illegal to open other people's mail, and I won't do it.' Connie threw the letters down on the floor. 'I won't.'

'Then he's going to kill you and Billy.' Cindy-Lou picked the letters up and put them in her own pile. She was silent for a while as she worked.

'Hey, I found money,' she said, holding up a dollar bill. 'In a birthday card for a kid in New York.'

'You must feel so proud,' said Connie before she could stop herself.

'Oh, don't you sit there judging me,' said Cindy-Lou petulantly. 'It's okay for you, being born into an educated family and able to teach children. Me and Artie, we got no skills. We got to make money for Baby Artie any way we can. To put food in his little belly.' There was something artificial about her speech, as if she had rehearsed it several times.

'You don't believe that, Cindy-Lou. You don't really want this sort of life for Baby Artie? Living in a cave, and only eating when Artie and the rest of Hunter's men can steal something?'

'We're not always going to be here. Hunter has big plans. Then we're all going over the border to Mexico, and living the good life.'

'What big plans?'

'I'm not allowed to say.'

'You might as well. I am aware of what Hunter does for a living.'

'It involves the bank in Ocasa. That's all I can say.'

'They're going to rob the bank? When?'

'I don't know. Soon, I guess. Hunter says it has to be done before the monthly salaries go out for Mr Truman's ranch hands. That's when there's the most in the bank.'

'Nate's money? They're going to steal Nate's money?'

'I guess. The whole payroll is in at this time of the month. Mr Truman is the only one in town who's really rich. The other farmers, they do okay, but Mr Truman makes a lot from his ranch and other business interests.'

'I suppose you found all this out while you were staying with him.'

Cindy-Lou looked sheepish again. 'I guess.'

'He helped you, Cindy-Lou. Put a roof over your head and Baby Artie's when you needed it. How could you steal from him? How could you help them arrange to take all his money like this?'

'I know he helped me. So did you. But Artie said I had to show where my loyalties lie. He's my man.'

'Not much of one,' Connie muttered, having given up all ideas of being tactful.

'Why ain't you working?' a voice said from the mouth of the cave. It was not

Hunter. The speaker stepped in, revealing himself as a tall and lanky youth. From what Connie could make out by the light from the fire, he had bad skin and bad teeth. Connie could definitely smell his body odour even from a distance.

'I am working, honey,' said Cindy-Lou.

'This is Artie?'

'Yes.' The girl beamed. 'This is my man. Ain't he wonderful?'

'Hmm,' said Connie through pursed lips.

'You Mrs Bradford?' asked Artie.

'Yes, that's right.'

'I wanna thank you for saving my boy. I didn't know they'd be on that train, Mrs Bradford, that's the truth. I'd never have done it otherwise.'

Connie's voice softened, but she spoke with urgency. 'If you truly care about them, Artie, why don't you get them away from here?'

'My place is at my pa's side. Frank and Artie Hunter, desperadoes.' Artie did not sound much older than Billy when he spoke like that.

'Hunter is your father?' Connie could only suppose that Artie took after his mother.

'Sure is. My ma left when I was little. So it's been me and my pa almost forever. Taught me everything he knows. I'm gonna teach my son the same.'

'Artie, you live in a cave! How can you want that for Baby Artie?'

'Hey, don't you go criticising, Mrs Bradford. You saved my boy's life and I owe you — but it don't give you no right to tell me how to raise him.'

'I'm sorry if I spoke out of turn,' Connie said hastily. 'But, Artie, if you really owe me, help me and Billy get away from here.'

'No way. My pa thinks that Mr Truman will pay good money for you.'

'Your pa is wrong, Artie. Mr Truman has no special feelings for me.'

'That's not what Cindy-Lou says.'

'Cindy-Lou is wrong. Artie, you can't keep two children in this cave. If you won't let Baby Artie go, at least take Billy home. He's frightened.'

'Pa says he's got to stay till we decide what to do with him.'

'So are you going to become a child killer because your father says so, Artie? Is that how you want your son to remember you?'

'Hey, look here, don't come with none of this here psycho . . . psych . . . mind-busting stuff. I got nothing to be ashamed of. This country gave me and my pa nothing, so we've gotta take it. You get to work, Mrs Bradford, or . . . or you'll be next.'

'Artie, please!' Cindy-Lou entreated. 'She saved our baby.'

'Yeah, well, maybe I'll repay her by letting her live, maybe I won't.'

'Big man,' Connie whispered.

'Hey, Artie!' Hunter called through the mouth of the cave. The light outside had gone completely so that his voice appeared to come from the blackest pit. 'We're going down to the town now it's dark, to work out how we're gonna take the bank. You take care of these here women and that child. Don't you let me down, now. Vernon is at the bottom of the ledge, on lookout, so no one will come up here.'

'Okay, Pa.'

Artie sat down next to Cindy-Lou and started whispering things in her ear that made her giggle.

'There is a child present,' said Connie, when she heard the direction the discussion was taking.

'Yeah, so what?' said Artie.

Connie had never wanted to harm anyone in her life. She was far too placid and kind. But more than anything she would have liked to slap Artie Hunter at that moment.

She tried to feel sorry for him. Nate would have probably grown up the same, had his father not died. Despite thinking it, she could not imagine it. Nate was intelligent, and that intelligence might have saved him even without a formal education. Artie was not just uneducated. He lacked basic comprehension.

This much became clear when he picked up one of the letters that Cindy-Lou had thrown to the floor and asked her to read it to him.

'Who sent this?' he asked.

'It says Doctor . . . ' Cindy-Lou squinted in the poor light. 'Doctor . . . I can't make out that name. It's from a place called Der-bye-shire.'

Connie started on hearing the name of her former home county.

'Is Derbyshire in America?' asked Artie.

'No, silly, it's in England.'

'How do you know it's in England?'

'Because it's on the map.'

'I can't read a map.'

'You can't read, full stop.' Cindy-Lou smiled at him indulgently.

'So how'd that letter get all the way from England?'

'It came by mail, of course. Across the sea.'

'Oh, yeah . . . on a boat.'

'Well it can't have come by train.' Cindy-Lou giggled. 'At least not until it reached America.'

'If it's from England, how come you can read it, Cindy-Lou?'

'Because it's in English, and that's what we speak.'

'I thought we talked American.'

'Can't you read, Artie?' asked Connie.

'No, I can't. Are you gonna make something of it?'

'No, I just thought that perhaps you might like to one day. So you can teach Baby Artie. I could teach you. Why not pass the letter to me and . . . '

'I don't need to learn to read. I got Cindy-Lou and my Pa to do that for me. You're thinking I'm not good enough because I got no learning . . . '

'No, I'm not thinking that at all. It's just that if you learned to read, you could teach Artie or read him stories.'

'Oh, we know stories,' said Artie proudly. 'Even if we can't read. Tales of the road.'

'Tell me one,' said Connie. 'I'm sure Billy would like to hear it, wouldn't you, Billy?'

She felt, rather than saw, the child

nodding his head. He was still clinging tightly to her.

'I know about Robin Hood,' said Artie. 'He stole from the poor and gave to the rich.'

'I think you'll find it's the other way around,' said Connie.

'Not the way my pa tells it.' Artie laughed at his own joke.

They lapsed into silence for at least an hour, whilst Cindy-Lou continued to work on opening the letters. From what Connie could make out, she had not found more than a couple of dollars.

Connie tried to think of another way to get the letter. If it came from Derbyshire, then it was possible it was for her and she longed to see it. They had known the local doctor very well. She did not know why he might be writing to her, as he had been Elizabeth and George's friend rather than hers, but it was a link with home.

But of course, he would not be writing to her. He would be writing to Elizabeth, because no one at home knew that Elizabeth had died.

Sitting in the dark cave, the night outside growing ever colder and the warmth from the fire doing nothing to raise the temperature, she suddenly felt very homesick. The Peak District had been her home all her life, and she might never see it again. She wished she had said no when Elizabeth asked if they should move to America. Her sister might still be alive. The journey had exhausted her. The rough sea crossing, and bad food and water they sometimes had on the way, would not have helped.

She pushed the painful memories aside and tried to concentrate on the matter in hand. It dawned on her that in all the time they had been sitting there, no one had checked on Baby Artie. As far as she knew, the child was alone in one of the upper caves. Yet she had not heard him cry in all that time. Then she saw a dark figure pass by the cave entrance, walking down the ledge, and realised that someone must have been with the child after all. That was something, at least.

'Artie,' she said eventually. 'About the letter . . . ' She was prevented from saying any more by a shrill whistle piercing the night.

'What the . . . ?' Artie stood up, almost banging his head on the roof of the cave, and went to the entrance. He peered around, and the shrill whistle sounded again. 'I think Vernon might be in trouble,' he said to Cindy-Lou. 'I'd better go down and see if he's okay.'

When Artie did not return after five minutes, Cindy-Lou began to get nervous. 'I can't help wondering what's happened to Artie. I think I'll . . . '

A dark form appeared in the cave entrance and she gasped in relief.

'Artie! You had me scared, honey. What was wrong with Vernon?'

'I think you'll find both Vernon and Artie sleeping off a headache.'

'Nate!' Delight flooded through Connie and she jumped up, forgetting about the low roof, so that her head scraped it.

She pulled Billy up from the floor and they staggered towards Nate.

'Come on, quickly,' said Nate. 'We don't have much time. Cindy-Lou, are you coming?'

'You hurt Artie!'

'It was either knock him out or kill him. Be grateful it wasn't the latter, Cindy-Lou. Now are you coming with us?'

'I'm not leaving here.'

'What about Baby Artie?' asked Connie urgently. 'Are you going to let him stay here? Let me take him, Cindy-Lou.' She hesitated to add that it was obvious the girl did not care about the child, not having checked on him for over an hour.

'You're not taking my baby from me.'

'I'm sorry,' said Nate, 'but we have to go. I left it as long as I could, until it was dark. We need to start climbing.'

'Climbing?' Connie looked up at him in surprise.

'Yep, climbing. You don't think I came in the front way like you did, did you? I went around the hill and up over the top. They're not looking that way, on account of the town not being in that direction. I've been sitting up there with Baby Artie. Now we have to go. Cindy-Lou?'

'What?' Cindy-Lou's voice was sullen.

'If you're not coming and you're not going to let us take Baby Artie, I suggest you come up and feed him and change his diaper. I did my best after Big Artie left the cave, but he needs his mother.'

Nate took Connie's hand, and it was the most wonderful feeling she had ever known. She and Billy would be safe now; she knew it.

'Come on, let's take Billy home to his ma and pa.'

They started walking up the ledge and as they passed the upper cave, she heard Baby Artie whimpering from within its depths.

'Nate, we can't leave the baby here.'

'We can't abduct him, either.' Nate turned to face her. 'From what I've overheard, he's Hunter's grandson, and that's going to bring a whole load of trouble to Ocasa.'

'I don't care. I'm not leaving that child alone in that cave.'

He sighed. 'Okay, I'll go and get him. You wait here.'

'You're not taking my baby!' They had not realised Cindy-Lou was behind them. 'I'm his mama and he's staying with me.' She brushed past them and went into the cave. 'It's all right, baby. Mama's here.'

Under the circumstances there was nothing Connie and Nate could do. He took her hand, and led her up around the ledge. Her heart was heavy, thinking of the life the child would have.

She felt Nate's hand squeeze hers.

'I'm sorry,' he whispered gently. 'I couldn't exactly wrestle him from his mama.'

'I know, Nate,' she answered dejectedly.

'And another thing,' he said a few seconds later, as if his mind had been following some other train of thought. ‘Why would you think I’d refuse to pay a ransom for you?’

She did not have an answer that would not reveal her feelings for him. ‘You’re not responsible for me,’ was all she could manage.

‘We’ll see about that.’

Nate led Connie and Billy along the ledge, which got narrower as they neared the top.

‘Do we have to climb the cliff?’ Connie asked anxiously.

‘Yep, but don’t worry. I’ve got a rope ready and it’s not too steep. It’s just around this corner.’

They had just reached the rope when they heard a commotion below them. Artie had regained consciousness — and was yelling down the hill towards Ocasa for his father.

14

Connie's shoulders felt as if they were being dragged from their sockets. Every muscle strained to keep up against the rock as she climbed, hand over hand, to the top. Billy, enthused by Nate's appearance and starting to enjoy his adventure again, had climbed the rope easily, and was waiting at the top for her and Nate.

Nate was just behind her, also climbing hand over hand. They could hear Cindy-Lou crying in the distance, and it sounded as if the girl was trying to cover for them.

'I don't know which way they went,' she was saying, as her shrill tones filled the night air. 'He said he'd shoot me and Baby Artie if I followed.'

'Nate . . . ' Connie whispered his name urgently.

'It's okay,' he whispered back. 'I think

she's just buying us time.'

'But to say you threatened to shoot the baby. It's unfair!'

'I can live with that, as long as we get away. Just climb, before they realise we came uphill.'

Connie strained to pull herself further up the rope. She had reached the top when she heard voices.

'There they are! He's on the rope. Shoot him.'

'Nate!' Connie pulled frantically on the rope, trying to hoist him up more quickly, but he was too heavy. 'Billy, help me.'

They tugged on the rope, trying hard to bring Nate to the top, but he was a large man and weighed more than both of them could manage.

He started climbing even faster when they heard Artie's voice at the bottom. Connie could not see him from where she was. It was too dark.

'Come back here!' the youth cried. 'Come back or I'll shoot.'

'Oh, Nate!'

'Just keep pulling,' growled Nate.

'Unless he can aim in the dark, he isn't going to get me.'

A shot rang out in the night, almost causing Connie to drop the rope. Several more shots followed. It seemed to take an age before Nate crawled over the top and into her waiting arms.

'Are you hurt?' she asked urgently, as he clung to her. Without thinking, she stroked his head.

'No. Just enjoying the sensation of your arms around me.'

'Behave in front of Billy,' she chided him.

'You're right. I forgot myself for a moment there. Forgive me, Billy.'

They felt a tug on the rope. Nate got up and reached into his pocket for a knife, which he used to cut the rope. They heard a thud and then Artie swearing loudly, followed by, 'Pa is going to kill me.'

'Come on.' Nate pulled Connie up from the ground. 'My horse is at the bottom of this hill. It's a long way down.'

That side of the hill was more remote

than the one leading up the caves. The land had not been cultivated, and there was less grass. By the time they reached the halfway mark, Billy was exhausted. Nate picked him up and carried him on his shoulders.

'Thank you for coming to save us,' said Connie humbly as she walked alongside them.

'I didn't.'

'Oh.' She was deflated. 'Well — I mean, for coming to save Billy.'

'No — what I mean is that I've been up there most of the day, waiting for the right time to get Billy. I got there before you did.' His tone changed and he became angry. 'What were you thinking, going up there alone? Damn it, they might have shot you before you reached the caves.'

'Someone had to. The townspeople were looking everywhere but up in the hills. You rode off in a huff . . . '

'A *huff?*' She heard him laughing in the darkness. 'A huff? Is that an English word?'

'In a mood. And I understand why

you did, because it was wrong of me to make you feel responsible.'

'Yes, it was.' They lapsed into silence for a while, because the downhill slope became harder to navigate.

'I'm sorry,' Connie whispered when they were on more even ground.

'No. I'm sorry you thought I let you down. I knew I was wrong five minutes after I rode away. So I had the idea of going in the back way. No one uses this pass, because it leads nowhere and then there's the drop to the cave. A posse wouldn't have made it without drawing attention to themselves, but one man on his own . . . That's a different thing. Hunter wasn't expecting that.'

'And you've been with the baby?'

'I was hiding at the back of the cave when Cindy-Lou put him in there. I'm sorry we couldn't bring him. I'm not sure we could have climbed the cliff carrying him anyway. We'll work out a way to get him, I promise.'

He reached out and took Connie's hand.

'Hunter is planning to rob the bank.'

'I know. I heard them planning it. We'll warn the sheriff and put an extra guard on it.'

'Will you ever forgive me for going up the caves?'

'Probably not.' He stopped walking. Connie could see his horse a few feet away. 'But I might, if you promise never to do anything that crazy again. Or climb into unstable carriages, for that matter.'

'You climbed down a cliff to save Billy. And it's only luck that Hunter and most of his men went down into town. So you were also planning to face them alone. What's the difference between what you did and what I did? Is it because you're a man?'

'Yes. Love makes a man unreasonable, especially where the safety of the woman he loves is concerned. Come on. Billy can sit in front of me and you can sit behind.'

Speechless, Connie climbed up onto the horse behind him and they rode back to Ocasa.

It took them over an hour to ride around the pass, by which time Billy was fast asleep and Connie was half-dozing with her head resting on Nate's back, feeling as if her heart was flying towards the town ahead of her. Had he really said he loved her? She clung a little tighter and was vaguely aware of his head turning slightly in response.

'Are you safe back there?'

'Oh yes,' she murmured. 'Safer than I've ever felt.'

'That's good to know.'

* * *

When they reached the town it was to find all the lights blazing, and a group of men standing in the main street carrying blazing torches.

'Hey, Joshua, what's happening?' called Nate, as they approached.

'We caught Hunter and his men. They're in jail. We're just on our way up the hill to get Mrs Bradford and

Billy . . . ' Joshua nearly dropped his torch. 'You've got him!'

'Yep. Hey, Billy.' Nate touched the boy's head. 'Your grandpa is waiting for you.'

Billy stirred and slid down off the horse into his grandfather's waiting arms. 'Oh my boy, my boy,' murmured Joshua, hugging the child close.

Billy's mother, Emma, emerged from the crowd, sobbing and calling for her child, closely followed by Paolo Estevez.

'I owe you, Mr Truman,' said Paolo when the reunion had calmed down a little. He reached up and shook Nate's hand.

'You owe me nothing. Just take care of your boy and keep him out of trouble in future.'

'I will.'

'You can do one thing for me,' said Nate. 'Leave Bernardo alone. He's not to blame for this.'

'It is okay, Mr Truman. We owe young Bernardo a huge debt. He told us Hunter was coming into town.

Where is he? Come here, Bernardo.'

The child had been standing quietly amongst the crowd, hidden from Connie's view. He stepped forward and meeting her eyes, waved shyly.

'Please do not be angry with me, Mrs Bradford. I went back. They did not see me because I am small, and they were too busy talking about you, so I heard their plans to come down to town and plan the bank robbery. I ran back to town to tell everyone.'

'We had a posse waiting,' added Joshua. 'Rounded them all up. Apart from the couple of lookouts he left up there.'

'That was a very brave thing to do, Bernardo,' said Connie. 'I'm very proud of you. But you should still have done as I asked. You might have been terribly hurt.'

'Look who's talking!' said Nate. He smiled down at the Hispanic boy. 'Come on, Bernardo. We'll take Mrs Bradford home, then take you back to the orphanage.'

'I am not going back to the orphanage,' said Bernardo, with a big beaming smile.

Paolo and Emma Estevez put their arms around the child. 'Bernardo is coming to live with us, to be Billy's brother,' said Paolo.

Billy smiled up at his father in delighted surprise.

'We think he will help keep our boy out of trouble. I owe him something for treating him so unkindly. I promise I will be a good father to him. I will treat him like my own.'

Connie felt tears prick her eyes. She was delighted for Bernardo's sake that he had a new family, but part of her had hoped that she might adopt him. She knew it was unlikely she would be allowed to, but she felt sad for chances lost. If only she had spoken up sooner.

'I'm so happy for you all,' she said, swallowing hard. Nate's hand covered hers as if he understood.

'Yeah, me too,' he said. 'You make sure you treat him well, Paolo. Remember he's just a kid, too. He's not Billy's keeper.'

She understood Nate was warning Paolo not to blame Bernardo for any other problems Billy might have, based on his father's previous indulgent treatment of the child.

'I am man enough to admit I got things wrong,' said Paolo, nodding. 'But I respect your warning. You want for the child what we want for him.'

Nate touched Connie's hand again. 'We'd better get you home.'

They were about to ride away when there was an almighty shout from the direction of the Youlgreaves' house.

'Help, someone!' cried the Reverend, running out of the garden gate wearing just his long-johns, looking very unlike his usual calm and collected self. 'Sofia has gone into labour. Help . . . '

* * *

Connie and Emma Estevez rushed in and out of Sofia's bedroom, bringing hot water and towels, as she lay on the bed crying out in Spanish. Connie had the distinct impression that some of the words were a bit risqué, judging by Emma's giggles.

Sofia was particularly vocal when Reverend Youlgreave came into the bedroom and asked, 'Are you well, my darling?'

'No. I am not well. I will not let you touch me again. You monster. To put your loving wife through this.'

'Shh,' Connie soothed, trying not to giggle. She placed a damp cloth on Sofia's brow. She had no idea if she was doing the right thing, having only once attended the birth of a local child with her mother.

'Try not to get upset, Sofia. Perhaps you should go and wait in the kitchen, Reverend.'

'What? If you think so, Mrs Bradford. This is women's work, after all.'

'Women's work!' cried Sofia. 'It is a curse, brought on by men, that is what it is.'

'I'll be in the kitchen,' said the Reverend. He looked so crestfallen that Connie wanted to hug him.

'You know you adore him really,' she said, as she helped Sofia into a more comfortable position.

'True. I adore him. But at this moment I hate him. It hurts so much. How could he do this to me, the woman he loves?'

It was a refrain that Connie and Emma Estevez were to hear several times over the next few hours.

As Connie was rushing back into the kitchen for more hot water, she overheard the Reverend saying to Nate, 'A confession would be helpful. Otherwise I'm not sure it would be legal, Nate. I imagine you want it to be all legal and above board.'

'I wouldn't settle for anything less.'

'Do you mean Hunter's men?' she said as she pushed open the kitchen door. 'Surely the fact that Bernardo overheard them is enough. Plus they have all the mail from the train up in the caves. That's evidence, isn't it?'

They sat at the table drinking coffee. Nate was badly in need of a shave, and yet Connie had never seen him look so attractive. He oozed masculinity, looking more like the man of the comic book legends than the grimy Hunter and his lanky son, Artie, ever could. The beauty of it was that Nate was a good, kind man, with a noble heart. And he had said he loved her!

Neither man spoke, and she became self-conscious about the way they watched her as she lifted the pan from the fireplace. 'Isn't it?' she pressed, to break the uncomfortable silence.

'Yes,' said Nate, eventually. He exchanged glances with the Reverend. 'I'd forgotten about the mail. You're right. That should be enough to convict Hunter of the train hijack even if we can't get him for the bank robbery.'

She smiled and returned to the bedroom. It was amazing how men thought they knew everything, and yet the obvious usually escaped them.

* * *

Sofia's baby girl was born at five o'clock in the morning. Emma cut the umbilical cord and Connie wrapped the child in a blanket, handing her to her mother.

'She is so beautiful,' Sofia sobbed. 'Where is my Christopher? Where is my love?'

The Reverend joined them, and clearly forgiven for his transgressions. 'She is beautiful,' he said, his eyes shining with happy tears. 'A beautiful, healthy girl. You are wonderful.' He kissed his wife so passionately that Connie and Emma both looked away, blushing.

Nate stood in the doorway, smiling. 'I think it's time I took you home,' he said to Connie. 'You look exhausted.'

'I am rather tired. Sofia, will you be able to manage?'

'I will, now I have my baby.'

'I'll stay till morning,' said Emma. 'What am I saying? It's already morning. I mean I'll stay till later today, in case I'm needed again.'

Connie reached over and kissed Sofia's head. 'Congratulations.' She kissed the Reverend on the cheek, shyly.

'Muchas gracias, querida. Muchas gracias,' Sofia said, teary-eyed. Connie had reached the door when Sofia called her back.

'I have not told you what we intend to name our princess. We are going to name her Constance. We like it so much, do we not, Christopher?'

'Yes, very much.'

Connie felt as though she had been hit with a sledgehammer.

'This upsets you, querida?' asked Sofia.

'No, no. It's wonderful that you should name her after my sister.'

She turned and all but ran from the house. She had reached the gate when Nate caught her by the arm.

'Hey, slow down. I'm supposed to be taking you home.'

'There's no need, really. I can find

my way from here. It's starting to get light and all Hunter's men are in jail.'

Connie needed to be alone, to think. She was in a quandary, brought about by fatigue and Sofia's innocent announcement of her baby's name. They had obviously believed it would please Connie. What it did was remind her how long she had lied to them. To all of them. Nate included.

'They're not all in jail,' he said now.

'They will be soon.'

'Soon is not now. Slow down. I know you're tired, but we have time to talk on the way.'

'Nate . . . please go home. I'm so exhausted, I don't even know if I can speak any more tonight. This morning. I haven't slept for nearly twenty-four hours, and neither have you.'

'Then we'll just walk and enjoy the morning air without talking.'

Despite Connie's protestations, he walked alongside her. Too tired to argue, she fell into silence.

What she really wanted was to ask

him to hold her. To tell her that things would be all right, and that it did not matter that she'd lied to everyone. But she had lied for too long. How could she tell the truth now?

The townspeople had trusted her with their children, as an arbiter of morals. What might they say now if they knew the truth? If she were honest, it was not the townspeople's reaction that really bothered her. It was what Nate would say that frightened her.

He had poured his heart out to her, told her everything about himself — and she had kept the most important truth from him. That she was not Elizabeth Bradford, widowed schoolteacher. She was an impostor, who took her sister's place. He had as much as told her he loved her. But what if that love was for the person he believed she was? Not for Constance Ruddick, but for Elizabeth Bradford?

'I think you should close the school today,' he remarked, as they neared her cottage. She nodded.

'Yes. I'm too tired to open it. But I need to tell everyone . . . '

'I'll do that. It won't take long for the word to get around Ocasa. You just go in and get some sleep.'

'Thank you.' She fought the compulsion to ask him to stay with her, to lie by her side and hold her tightly. He would probably be shocked. She was a little shocked that it occurred to her, but she longed to feel his arms around her. Then she could tell him the truth — and if he did not want to know her, at least she would have that memory.

'Nate,' she murmured.

'What?'

'Will you kiss me, please?'

It was the most daring thing she had ever asked a man, but it seemed at that moment as if her life depended on him kissing her.

He pulled her into his arms and kissed her so tenderly that a sob caught in her throat. She clung to him, and very nearly begged him to stay, afraid that it might be the only time.

He let her go slowly, and wiped a stray tear from her cheek.

'I've never had a woman cry when I kissed her before.'

'It was a wonderful kiss,' she whispered. 'I only wish . . . '

'What do you wish?'

Blushing, she lowered her head. 'I think it's probably best if you go now. Before I make an even bigger fool of myself.'

'You could never do that with me. Remember that, when you're wrestling with the thing that's bugging you.'

She looked up at him sharply. 'What do you mean?'

He stroked her cheek. 'I mean that things won't seem so bad when you're rested. I promise.'

Connie went to her front door then turned back. 'Nate . . . '

'What is it, darling?'

'Whatever happens, I want you to know that I love you.'

15

There was a definite party atmosphere as Connie walked through the streets of Ocasa with a basket full of flowers and foliage. Bunting hung from the buildings and happy children ran through the streets yelling and laughing. The town band were standing on the porch near Old Tom's store, practising a cheerful mariachi tune. Some of the children shouted hello to her as she passed them, happy to have been given yet another day's holiday from school so they could attend the carnival. She saw Bernardo and Billy sitting next to each other on the sidewalk, watching all the excitement.

'Good morning, boys.'

'Good morning,' they both chirruped.

'You look very pretty today, Mrs Bradford,' said Bernardo.

'Why thank you kind sir,' she said,

smiling and nodding her head in a courtly fashion.

'I bet Mr Truman thinks so,' said Billy. Judging by his and Bernardo's reaction, this was the funniest thing Billy had ever said. They fell backwards laughing.

'Good morning, Mrs Bradford,' Tom called as she passed by his store.

'Good morning, Tom. How are you today?'

'All the better for seeing you, Mrs Bradford. All the better for seeing you. It's nice to see those young 'uns getting on so well, ain't it? I always said that Bernardo was a good boy.'

Connie was in too good a mood to contradict him. What Nate had said several weeks before had been true. She'd felt much better after a good sleep. She had decided that she had overreacted to the announcement of Sofia's baby's name. It was a kind gesture, nothing more.

'I'm sure you did, Tom,' she said.

'Won't have a word said against the boy!'

'Well, Mrs Bradford,' said Mr Fletcher, who stood in the bank doorway. 'You really are a picture today.'

Connie feared that she would be very bigheaded by the end of the day with all the compliments she received. So she just smiled a thank you and walked on. Mr Fletcher had not bothered her about signing the documents for a few weeks, and that suited her. She supposed that with the worries about an attack on the bank, he had bigger concerns. The town committee had been meeting to discuss better security measures, and Mr Fletcher's time was taken up with that.

When she reached the far end of town, Sofia came from the vicarage, carrying little Constance in her arms. 'Querida, there you are! Come, we must go and decorate the carriages.'

They had been put in charge of adorning a dozen carriages with flowers, each one representing a different part of the town's history and commerce; the orange growing, the Spaniards arriving in the fourteenth century, the gold mines, and some historical moments in the town that Connie had not known much about until recently.

The carriages were waiting up at the schoolhouse, and once adorned would start their journey down through the town, turning at the end of the main street, before coming back up the school to be placed in a circle around an outdoor dining area set up in the school playground. Happy little girls, wearing pure white dresses, and with flowers in their hair, sat on the school porch, waiting for the moment when they would sit aloft the carriages and be princesses for a day.

'I feel as if the clouds have lifted from Ocasa,' declared Sofia, as she placed her daughter on top of a soft blanket in the back of the carriage they were decorating. She lifted up the tailgate, so that the baby could not roll out. 'Now that Hunter and his men are on their way to a federal prison, and the railroad is open again. We can all get on with our lives. Is it not wonderful, querida?'

'Yes, it is,' said Connie. She started to take flowers from her basket and fix them to the carriage. 'It's wonderful. I just wish I knew what happened to Cindy-Lou and Baby Artie.'

'Christopher said that when the men went up into the hills, the caves were deserted. They only found the mail sacks.'

'Oh . . . '

'What is it, querida?'

'Cindy-Lou mentioned that there was a letter from Derbyshire, and I wondered if it was for me. But Big Artie wouldn't let me look at it. I wonder if it's amongst the letters the men found.'

'We must ask them to look. It will be good to hear from home, si?'

'Yes, yes, it would. Though . . . I feel as though Ocasa is my home now I'm so happy here, Sofia. I can't begin to tell you . . . '

'You do not have to, querida. I can see it in your face. And in Senor Truman's whenever he comes to town.'

Connie blushed. 'I've barely seen him over the past few weeks. We've all been so busy.'

Their meetings had been fleeting, but very sweet and innocent — even if Connie's feelings for him were anything but sweet and innocent. He treated her like a delicate flower. Sometimes she wanted to tell him he did not have to, but drew back, fearing the consequences of her boldness. In England there were external checks on such behaviour, with villagers voicing their disapproval at any outward show of emotion.

The people of Ocasa, with their Hispanic ancestry, were not so closed about their emotions. Some of that seemed to have rubbed off onto Connie. At least whenever she was in Nate's company. It would not be the worst thing in the world for her to become like Sofia — she loved her friend dearly — but one passionate, outspoken woman in Ocasa was probably as much as the town would cope with.

'What are you smiling about?' asked Sofia, coming to Connie's side of the carriage and putting her arm around her waist.

'You! I was just thinking that I'm becoming more like you. Which is both wonderful and terrifying in equal measure. Much as you are, my darling friend.'

Sofia laughed. 'Ah, that is because you are in love with Senor Truman, querida, as I am in love with Christopher. Do not deny it. Everyone knows.'

Connie beamed, and as she did so her smile grew wider still. Nate was walking up the hill towards the school.

'Good morning,' he said, tipping his hat to both ladies.

'Good morning, Nate.'

'Good morning, Senor Truman. You cannot take her yet. We need her help.' Sofia pouted theatrically before her face broke into a huge smile.

'I just wandered up here to admire the view,' he said, looking directly at Connie. 'You'll all be coming to dinner at the ranch tonight, won't you?'

'Yes, of course,' said Connie.

'I've opened up the ballroom too, and asked the band to join us so that we can dance.'

'Oh how exciting!' Sofia clapped her hands together. 'I will find someone to sit with Constance. I have not danced for far too long now.'

As if realising that Connie and Nate wanted to talk privately, Sofia moved back to the other side of the carriage. 'I am still chaperoning you from here,' she teased, as she began fixing flowers again.

'You look beautiful,' Nate said to Connie in a low voice.

'You look very handsome yourself.'

'You're missing something, though.'

'What?' Connie looked down at her clothes, wondering what was wrong with the white dress and red sash that she wore.

Nate took a flower from her basket, and fixed it in her hair. She swayed towards him, thrilled by his touch.

'Now that's perfect,' he whispered. He bent down and kissed her lightly on the lips.

'All the demons gone away?' he asked, placing his hand on her shoulder. He stroked the bare skin above her collar with the edge of his thumb, sending a myriad of sensations coursing through her body.

'Yes.'

'Good. I want to talk to you later. Alone, if possible.'

'Is something wrong?'

'Not from where I'm standing. But what I've got to say is for your ears only.' His lips brushed her cheek, and she half-turned her head to meet them with her own lips.

'I'll see you tonight,' she whispered.

'You'll see me all day.'

'You know what I mean.' Connie blushed.

'Is that a promise?' He made the word sound like a seduction.

'Yes. To talk, I mean.'

'Of course. To talk.' His lips twisted

slightly at the corners.

'Stop it!'

'I'm not doing anything. Look, here are both my hands.'

'It's what you're thinking that worries me.'

'That's entirely your fault for looking the way you do,' he whispered. He backed away, revealing a very wicked grin. He waved to everyone and began walking back down towards the town.

'I was watching you,' called Sofia, smiling knowingly. 'You had better be good to my querida.'

'Don't you worry, Senora Youlgreave, I will.' Nate turned back briefly. 'And that is a promise.'

* * *

Soon the carriages were all ready. The little girls climbed excitedly onto the back, and the drivers began the descent down through the town, with the band leading them. Sofia had climbed up onto one of the carriages with her daughter, and was waving excitedly to everyone. She had not been invited to do so, but no one ever argued with Sofia and everyone smiled and cheered when they saw her.

Connie and the other women had gone on ahead so that they could watch the procession. Once it passed, they made their way back up to the schoolroom to prepare the lunch, whilst the men stood around talking business and the children cheerfully ran riot — but under the watchful eye of the adults, who checked any behaviour that might cause harm.

Outside in the school yard, a large grill cooked enormous steaks. A huge pot of chilli cooked on an open fire. The tables were laden with hot bread, and fresh fruit. The aroma made everyone's mouth water, and the fresh air and excitement gave them all good appetites. Even Old Tom had closed his store and made the trip up to the schoolyard. He sat at the end of one of the trestle tables, waited on hand and foot by some of the children as he told them tales of Ocasa in the olden days, before the railroad.

'What a great day for Ocasa,' Joshua Stephenson declared, when he decided to give an impromptu speech on the school porch. 'Hunter and his men are behind bars. The others with them have fled, and Ocasa is no longer in the grip of fear. The railroad is open again.' This was greeted by a loud cheer. 'And the Stephensons and Estevezes also have much to thank God for. My grandson, Billy, who was returned safe to us and the arrival in our family of two new members — Bernardo, who is a fine boy, and now little Constance. And if I'm not entirely mistaken, we may well hear wedding bells soon.'

Everyone laughed, and it was a moment before Connie realised that everyone was looking at her and Nate. 'Course,' Joshua continued, 'it probably means we'll have to find a new schoolmarm.' More laughter.

'Thanks, Joshua,' said Nate, laughing.

'I was going to ask her privately later, but since we're all together . . . ' He turned to Connie. 'Will you do me the honour of becoming my wife?'

'Oh . . . ' Connie was momentarily rendered speechless. Realising that the whole town was waiting breathlessly for her reply, she stammered, 'Er . . . yes. Yes, I will!'

The crowd cheered as Nate swept her into his arms and kissed her. He lifted her off the ground and spun her around.

'You just made me the happiest man alive,' he said.

'You can't possibly be happier than I am,' said Connie. She hugged him tight, tears of joy filling her eyes. Yes, everything would be well now.

Except that her overwhelming love and happiness had made her forget the most important stumbling block to marrying Nate. That she was not really Elizabeth Bradford.

Later that night, she was to be given a stark reminder.

16

Nate stayed at her side for the rest of the day, as they accepted the congratulations of nearly everyone in Ocasa. By the time Nate's guests started making their way up to his ranch for dinner, Connie's face hurt from smiling so much. Not that she complained. After the pain and darkness of the past few years, losing first her parents, then Elizabeth's husband George, then Elizabeth herself, she was finally happy again. Life felt good — and, more importantly, she was going to spend the rest of it with the man she adored.

The ranch had changed almost beyond recognition. No longer did it have the atmosphere of a dusty mausoleum in memory of Melissa Truman. Every part of it sparkled, and Nate had set his men to repainting it both outside and in, brightening the rooms and bringing them to life.

'It's wonderful, Nate,' she murmured

when she saw the ballroom, glittering with candles. The other guests were sitting in the drawing room, having tactfully allowed the young couple to be alone for a while.

'We'll have parties here every week,' he said, spinning her around.

'Not every week. I would rather like to keep you to myself sometimes. Is that selfish of me?' she asked, uncertainly.

'Only if it makes me selfish too, darling. Because that's what I want. Until we have children, that is.'

Connie blushed scarlet and made a great show of admiring the décor so that she did not have to look at his wicked eyes. 'I wish . . . I wish our sisters were here to see this,' she said, a sudden feeling of sadness overwhelming her. It had been a long day so perhaps it was natural that they should reach an anticlimax. But even then, she was not thinking of the problems ahead. She was only remembering Elizabeth and Melissa as being important to them both.

'I'm sure they're up there, nodding their approval,' he said, gently.

She turned back to face him and nodded. 'Yes, they will be. I know it.'

'Actually,' said Nate, 'I wanted to talk to you about your sister.'

At that moment, Sofia burst into the ballroom, excitedly. She wore a ball gown of deep scarlet, which only she could carry off with her wonderful skin tone. 'Oh — this is beautiful, beautiful. Am I interrupting?'

'No,' said Connie.

'Yes,' said Nate, looking a little annoyed. He appeared to remember his manners. 'But I couldn't imagine a more charming interruption, Senora Youlgreave.'

'Is the right answer. Everyone else they say, leave the young lovers alone. But I am responsible for this girl, Nathan Truman and I will be until the day you make an honest woman of her. Her sister is not here to protect her, so I will take her place.'

'I assure you my intentions are

honourable,' answered Nate.

'Your intentions might be, but your eyes when you look at her, they are not. Now, shall we all dance before dinner? Si?'

The rest of the evening passed in a daze of dancing, fine wine, good food, and more dancing. It was nearly midnight before everyone started to say goodnight.

'I'll take you home,' Nate said to Connie, when she almost fell asleep on his shoulder as they were dancing.

'No, no,' said Sofia, who stood nearby. 'Christopher and I will see her home. It is not proper, now you are engaged.'

'I don't remember you worrying too much about the conventions when we met,' said Reverend Youlgreave with a smile.

'I was more worldly than this child. I knew how to handle men like Senor Truman.'

'So the truth comes out at last,' said the Reverend, his eyes twinkling.

'You know I do not mean that. You are my one and only love.' She waved her husband away with her hand. 'Come, querida, you must sleep. Tomorrow we will find material for your wedding dress. When are you getting married? Have you set the date?'

'Soon,' said Nate. Connie could not help noticing that he and the Reverend exchanged glances. 'It might be easier to arrange it if we could be alone to discuss it.'

'There is nothing to discuss,' said Sofia. 'It can happen next week.'

'Next week?' Connie laughed. 'Please give me time to get my breath back, Sofia.'

'You two need to be married soon,' Sofia said, sagely. 'Christopher, you will arrange it, querido.'

'I seem to have no choice,' said the Reverend, but he looked troubled. Connie began to fear that he disapproved of the match between her and Nate, and wondered why. But he smiled at her warmly enough and with what seemed to be genuine affection.

It was some time later that Sofia and the Reverend left Connie at her cottage. She waved goodnight to them and went inside, lighting the candle on the table and setting light to the kindling on the fire. She was exhausted, and thought to go straight to bed, but she also longed for a quiet cup of coffee, sitting in her rocking chair. The day had been full of excitement, love and laughter, and she wanted to think about it for a while, before sleep took her. She especially wanted to think about Nate, in the hopes that if he was on her mind whilst she was awake, she would also dream about him.

* * *

She heard the sound outside half an hour later, as she rocked gently, lulling herself into a doze.

'Nate!' She stood up and went to the door. It did not matter what Sofia thought. She loved him and she wanted to be in his arms. They were going to be married. He had promised, in front of the whole town. So what difference did it make if they were alone together, late at night, in her cottage?

She opened the door, saying teasingly as she did so, 'There's no need to act as guard now that all Hunter's men are . . . '

Her smile faded. It was not Nate.

'Cindy-Lou.'

The girl stood on the porch, bedraggled and dirty.

'Hello . . . Miss Ruddick.'

An icy finger trailed down Connie's spine. 'What did you say?'

'I need money.'

'Very well,' said Connie resignedly. 'You'd better come in. I've only got a few dollars but . . . '

'No.' Cindy stayed where she was, as if she feared a trap. 'We need more money than that. Me and Artie need to go east with our baby before they catch Artie and put him in jail with his pa, but we got no money now they took all the mail back. We ain't eaten for days.'

'I don't have that much money, Cindy-Lou.' Connie's first thought was for the child.

'No, but your dead sister does. In the bank.'

'How do you know about that?' Her legs had turned to water.

'The letter from the doctor. Artie's got it. It was addressed to Constance Ruddick and said that he heard her sister Elizabeth had died. I knew then that you'd lied to everyone. Now we need money. You have to go and sign for it.'

'I can't do that, Cindy-Lou. It's fraud.'

'Then we'll tell everyone that you lied to them. Including your fiancé. That's fraud too.'

'I haven't broken any laws,' Connie said, her throat constricted. That was not the point, and she knew it. She may not have broken civil laws, but she had broken moral laws. It had been bad enough when she lied to the townspeople as a single woman. Now the deceit would reflect on Nate too, making a fool of him.

'Very well,' said Connie, coming to an instant decision. 'Come back here at the same time tomorrow night, and I'll have the money for you. But I want the letter. You can't keep coming back and blackmailing me.'

Cindy-Lou nodded. 'I'm really sorry about this, but . . . '

'Don't insult me with your apology, Cindy-Lou. People cared about you and your baby. Maria, Nate Truman — they would have taken care of you both. And I . . . I saved his life!' She looked at the girl in contempt. 'I think that after tomorrow I'll be happy never to see you again.'

'I never lied to anyone about who or what I was,' Cindy-Lou said, with tears splashing from her eyes. 'I may have stolen from Mr Truman, but I didn't work my way into his life and get him to promise to marry me, pretending to be someone else.'

With those savage words, Cindy-Lou

might just as well have stabbed Connie through the heart.

'Just go. I'll have the money for you tomorrow night.' She slammed the door in the girl's face, and ran to her bedroom, flinging herself onto the bed as a torrent of tears erupted.

* * *

In the early hours, she sat down to write a letter. It began: *Nate, I am sorry to say that I cannot marry you. I have been deceiving you all along and about many things* . . .

Every word was a dagger in her heart, but she had to save his pride, even if she could not save her own. She set down the truth about Elizabeth and tried to explain why she had taken her place. The townspeople would rally around him and sympathise about the impostor who had, as Cindy-Lou put it, worked her way into his life.

At the end, she wrote in what she hoped was a businesslike manner,

Furthermore, I find I do not love you, only to feel that having told him the truth, she could not tell that lie. She scored the words out and signed the letter in her own name.

At sunrise, she walked down to the town, carrying only a small bag, and went to the station.

'Going somewhere, Mrs Bradford?' asked the guard.

Connie bought a ticket for the town forty miles north. 'I'm going to find some fabric for my wedding dress. I thought I would go early, and enjoy the whole day. I've never managed to go there.' She realised she was rambling, and she hoped that the guard would not ask why she had not purchased a return ticket. When she reached the northern town, she would find another train to take her further west. She did not have much money, but she did have more than she had let on to Cindy-Lou the night before, having just been paid her monthly salary. After that, she would have to find work.

Her hope was that at some point she would earn enough to buy her passage home to England. Home seemed a long way away, and her only plan thus far was to leave Ocasa and Nate behind. She had not thought much beyond that.

'Are you okay, Mrs Bradford? You look as if you're about to cry there.' The guard handed her the ticket, gazing at her in concern.

'I think I'm getting a touch of hay-fever,' she said, sniffing. 'I do tend to suffer greatly with it in the summer.'

It might have helped if her voice had not broken on the last words.

She hurried onto the platform and was relieved to see that the train was already approaching the station. She would not have to wait there under the increasingly watchful eye of the guard.

The train was practically empty when she boarded it. A few itinerant workers from further south slept with their hats pulled down over their heads, and a couple of travelling salesman sat opposite each other playing cards. Connie stood looking out through the window of the carriage door, as the train started up and Ocasa disappeared into the distance behind them. When she could no longer see the orange groves on the hillside, she found a seat facing the other way, and settled down for her journey into loneliness.

Only the day before, she had been the happiest woman alive. Now that was all gone. She told herself that she had no alternative. Had she done as Cindy-Lou asked, and signed the document at the bank, her deceit would have been much worse.

How could she have married Nate with a criminal act hanging over her head? She was not entirely sure that she had not committed a crime of sorts. Had taking the salary meant for Elizabeth constituted a crime? She had earned it, and thought that the townspeople were happy with her work at the school, but it might still have been wrong to do so under a false name.

If only she had been honest from the outset. She might have had to turn straight round and return home, but at least then she would not have known what it was to love and be loved by Nate Truman. She would spend her whole life loving him — and the pain of knowing that, as well as knowing that she would now never see him again, seemed unbearable.

Swallowing hard, she struggled not to cry. She did not want to attract the attention of the other passengers. When he read her letter, he would hate her. As much as it hurt, she hoped that he would. That would make it easier for him to get over her and find someone else to love.

A small sob escaped her throat. One of the salesmen looked across at her. 'Are you all right, Ma'am?'

'Yes, thank you. Hayfever.'

'Oh yeah, it can get you real bad this time of year.' He did not sound as if he believed her.

* * *

They had been travelling for about half an hour when the train pulled to a stop.

'Darn it, not bandits again,' said the other salesmen. 'I thought they were putting better security on the train.'

No one boarded the train for a long time until, nearly another half an hour later, a horse and buggy sped past the window. This was followed by a commotion near the front of the train.

'Coming through!' someone shouted. 'Ah, there she is.'

Connie looked up to see Nate standing at the entrance to the carriage. A guard stood with him. 'Thanks for stopping,' he said to the guard.

'We didn't have much choice when they sent the signal up.'

'We meet again, Kitty Larue.' It took a moment for Connie to realise Nate was addressing her.

'What?'

Everyone in the carriage looked towards her.

'Excuse me, folks. This lady is under arrest.' Nate pointed to a sheriff's badge on his shirt. 'Kitty Larue, the meanest, darndest woman you ever met.'

'She sure looks innocent enough,' said the first salesman.

'Appearances can be deceptive,' returned Nate. He had reached Connie's side, and stretched out to take her arm. 'She's ensnared men up and down the country, then stolen from them.'

'She sure is pretty enough for that,' remarked the second salesman. 'It shows you can't be too careful nowadays.'

'I am not Kitty Larue,' protested Connie. 'And I am not coming with you. I'm going home.'

'Exactly. You're coming home. Now do I have to carry you from the train?' Nate sounded as if he meant business.

Connie thought about it for a moment. 'I'll walk.' She flushed scarlet as she walked past the other passengers with her head held high. She could hear the salesmen muttering to each other.

'I wouldn't mind being snared for a

short time,' one of them said. They started laughing together.

'Nope, that'd be a pretty little snare worth getting caught up in.'

* * *

Nate's horse and buggy were waiting outside the train. He lifted her onto the seat, and climbed up next to her, moving her along the bench.

'Am I really under arrest?' she asked.

'You're certainly not escaping,' he said, mysteriously. He pulled on the reins and turned the carriage so they were facing Ocasa. The horse sped up into a gallop, bouncing the buggy over the rocky ground.

'I didn't break the law . . . at least, I don't think I did. Cindy-Lou wanted me to by signing for the money, but I couldn't do it. I thought it was best just to go. Please let me go, Nate.'

'You find you don't love me?' he said, looking sideways at her. 'You find you don't love me?'

'I crossed that out.'

'Not well enough. When I saw those words, my heart broke. Do you have any idea how much you've hurt me today? And not just today. About everything.'

'I'm sorry I lied about being Elizabeth.'

'Before we get on to that, tell me why you crossed those words out. I want the truth.'

'You know I do love you, and I couldn't lie to you. Not about that.' A hot tear splashed onto Connie's cheek. 'I know I shouldn't have lied to you before . . .'

'I've known since the beginning who you really were.'

'What?' She stared at him.

'I kinda guessed it when you turned up at the schoolhouse. I saw a kindred spirit in you, someone who needed family and a home. But I wasn't sure. Then you told me that *Great Expectations* was a gift from your father. The inscription says *To my darling daughter, Constance*. Remember?'

'Oh. Yes. I remember.' Only she had not at that time, overwrought by the scene at the bank.

'And if that hadn't told me the truth, the first time I kissed you certainly did. Now, unless good old reliable George had problems in that direction, I'd say you'd never been kissed before in your life.'

'Was it so awful?'

'It was the sweetest kiss I've ever known. But we're getting off the subject. I've been waiting for you to trust me, as I trusted you. Each time I tried to get you to tell the truth, you backed away or Sofia interrupted us. If you love me, Constance . . . '

'Connie . . . no one but Father called me Constance.'

'Connie. If you love me, why didn't you trust me? That's all I wanted.'

'I was afraid, and the longer the lie went on, the worse it became. Then when Cindy-Lou arrived and pointed out that the truth would not only damage me, but you too . . . I couldn't stay. And I certainly could not go to the bank and commit fraud. Please just let me go, Nate. I can't bear to face anyone.'

17

Nate ignored her and continued on to Ocasa. 'Do you want to punish me? Is that it?' she asked when she saw the town coming into view. 'Very well, then. Take me to the sheriff, have me arrested.'

He looked sideways at her and smiled. 'I'm not taking you the sheriff.' True to his word, he drove through the main street of Ocasa and past the Sheriff's office.

'I see you found her,' called out Old Tom when they passed his store.

'Yep, Tom. I surely did.'

'Good work, Mr Truman. Good work.'

'Are we going to the bank?' asked Connie. 'To see Mr Fletcher? I haven't done anything. I didn't sign the paperwork.'

Nate drove past the bank, too.

Instead he drove on and stopped outside the Youlgreaves' house.

'Reverend!' he called. He went around to Connie's side and helped her down. She almost fell against him, finding that her legs would not carry her.

The Reverend and Sofia came from the house.

'Oh, you found her!' cried Sofia. 'That is wonderful.'

Nate practically marched Connie through the garden gate to where the Reverend and his wife waited.

'Tell the Reverend your real name,' Nate ordered.

'Nate, please . . . '

'Tell him!'

'I'm so sorry,' murmured Constance. 'I lied to you. I'm not Elizabeth Bradford. I'm her sister, Constance Ruddick. I only lied because I had nowhere else to go and I was afraid you wouldn't let me stay and . . . '

To her surprise both the Reverend and Sofia clapped their hands together and started laughing. Sofia pulled Connie into her arms, and hugged her fiercely.

'At last,' said Sofia.

'Thank the Lord for that,' said Reverend Youlgreave.

'You knew?' gasped Connie.

'Of course we knew, querida,' said Sofia. 'You are clearly not twenty-eight years old, for a start. Then there was all the fuss you made about signing the bank documents! Intelligent women like you do not nearly faint when faced with legal documents.'

'Does everyone know? In the town, I mean?'

'Just us and Nate,' said the Reverend. 'We've been waiting for you to trust us enough to tell the truth.' He looked almost as hurt as Nate had.

'I'm sorry. But as I said to Nate, the longer it went on, the harder it was to confess. I thought you would all hate me for lying to you.'

'I trust this settles things,' said Nate. Connie realised he was talking to the Reverend.

'Of course. All legal and above board, as I requested and as you wanted, Nate.'

'Good, then you can marry us now. This minute. Before she runs off to catch another train out of Ocasa.'

'What?' Connie turned to him. 'You still want to marry me?'

'More than anything.'

She shook her head. 'No. I can't marry you.'

Nate's face turned ashen. 'What, because you 'find you don't love me'? Is that it?'

'No, that's not it. I've never loved anyone in the way I love you. But you don't love me. Not really. You love Elizabeth Bradford, widowed school-teacher. Not Constance Ruddick. You don't know the real me. I've almost forgotten who I really am, I've been pretending for so long.'

'Were you Elizabeth Bradford when you climbed into the carriage to save Baby Artie?'

'No, I suppose not.'

'And were you Elizabeth Bradford when you walked all the way up the hill into a nest of bandits to save young Billy's life?'

'No.'

'So were you Elizabeth Bradford when I first kissed you and you kissed me back?'

'No, of course not.' Connie blushed, remembering that Sofia and the Reverend were listening to every word. 'I was me.'

'Then it's definitely you I love and want to marry.'

'You could have told me you weren't going to have me arrested, instead of making me suffer. I suppose you intended to punish me.'

'No. I was afraid that if I told you my intentions you'd demand I put you back on the train. But I promise you that from the minute we're married you won't be able to escape from Ocasa.'

Connie smiled through happy tears. 'I promise I'll never want to.'

* * *

She had to spend an agonising hour as Sofia fussed over her and insisted in dressing her properly for her wedding. Connie would have been happy to go to the church as she was, and she did not think Nate minded, but Sofia was adamant that even in a rush, things had to be done properly. 'This was my mother's wedding dress and her mother before her,' said Sofia. It was a dress of antique lace, with a frilled neckline and a tight waist. 'Oh, you look beautiful. Beautiful.'

Connie looked at herself in the mirror. The dress was lower cut than any she had ever worn, but she felt like a princess and in that moment she was glad Sofia had insisted on doing things the right way.

She walked up the aisle of the little church to the side of her handsome husband-to-be, to find that Old Tom and Mr Fletcher had been roped in as last-minute witnesses.

'It's kind of a rush,' Old Tom muttered, and Connie blushed when she saw him staring at her stomach. That was probably what everyone would think, she thought wryly.

Nate took her hand, and the Reverend began the service. 'Do you, Constance Ruddick . . . '

'Eh?' said Old Tom. 'Ruddick, you say?'

Connie looked up at Nate to see him smiling down at her, and it no longer mattered what people thought. All that mattered was that she was going to be married to the man she loved.

* * *

'Did you sleep well?' asked Nate, snuggling up to her in the bed, curving his body to hers. Outside the bedroom window, they could see the latter part of the pink tinged sunset. Connie had managed to miss another one, but for reasons that made her smile ecstatically.

'Eventually,' she said. 'When you let me.'

'Complaining?'

She turned to face him, and kissed his chin. 'Oh no. Not at all. I love you, Nate Truman.'

'I love you, Mrs Truman.'

She smiled blissfully and kissed him. 'Now at last I know who I am.'

'No more escape plans?'

'No. I'm happy to remain imprisoned here for the rest of my life.'

'Right here?'

She giggled. 'Yes, here. In this bed. Though . . . I know this is not very romantic, but I am a little hungry.'

'We'll go and see if Maria can rustle up some food for us.'

After a not very brief interlude, they made their way downstairs, and sat close together in the dining room, eating. They talked for a while about what they planned to do with their lives now they were married, and then sat in blissful silence.

It was during this silence that Connie thought she heard a sound outside. She got up and went to the front door. On opening it, she found a basket outside, in which lay Baby Artie, crying quietly. There was a note pinned to his chest. Connie picked him up in her arms.

Dear Miss Ruddick . . . though I guess I should call you Mrs Truman now. I'm sorry for what I did. Big Artie made me do it. I know that's no excuse, but it's the best one I've got. I'm glad you're happy now. You're a nice lady so you deserve to be. I know I have no right to ask any favours of you, but please take care of Baby Artie for me. I know you'll keep him safe and give him a good life. I love him, but I can't make sure he's safe. Not with the life me and Big Artie lead. Knowing how you love Mr Truman, I think you'll understand why I have to be with my man.

Yours, Cindy-Lou.'

'Oh, you poor darling,' she said to Baby Artie, rocking him gently. She was not sure she did understand Cindy-Lou putting Big Artie before her baby, but she did understand how overwhelming love could be.

As she turned to go indoors, she was sure she saw someone move behind a tree along the lane. But when she looked again, they seemed to have disappeared. Had Cindy-Lou waited long enough to see that her baby was safe?

Nate was waiting for her in the hallway. 'Looks like the stork got here sooner than the townspeople thought,' he observed with a wry smile.

'Can we take care of him, Nate? Please.'

'I've got a feeling that even if I said no, you'd ignore me,' he laughed.

'No, I wouldn't. This is something we both have to agree to, for his sake and for ours. I realise that I'm asking an awful lot, darling, but he doesn't have anyone else. We've got so much love in us to give him.'

Nate moved towards her, and stroked the baby's head in a way that was achingly paternal.

'Okay, but for now can I be a little bit selfish? Will you let Maria take care of him just for a day or two? It isn't normally the done thing to have a baby sharing your honeymoon and I would like you all to myself for a little while. Then I promise I'll be the best daddy in the world to Baby Artie and any other children the stork might bring.'

Connie smiled and blushed. 'I'll take him to her. Then, I promise — I'll be all yours.'

She took the baby to Maria, who was delighted to be caring for the child again. Connie returned to Nate, who was waiting in the drawing room, standing with his back to the fireplace, with his sister's picture up above him. Connie did not know whether she imagined it, but Melissa's wan smile seemed wider, happier.

'Thank you,' she said, reaching up to kiss him. 'Now I know that Melissa and Elizabeth will be smiling down on us.'

His arms enfolded her.

'You don't have to thank me. There's no way I'd have sent the baby away, either. But if I needed to be reminded why I love you, Constance Ruddick Truman, you've just shown me the reason.'

She stretched up and whispered in his ear, 'And I love you because you're just like the man Jesse James should have been.'

THE END

Other titles in the Linford Romance Library:

TAKE A CHANCE ON ME

Teresa Ashby

A marathon brings doctors Anna Curtis and Riordan 'Mac' McKenna together. Anna has moved into the area with her late sister's little boy, Cameron, and Mac offers her a job at his surgery. They become close and Anna falls pregnant. However, when Mac's ex-wife informs her that he doesn't want children, she decides she must move away. Can Mac finally convince her that he loves her, Cameron and the baby?

LOVE IS ALL AROUND

Beth James

When Holly and Granny Jean embark on a round-Britain cruise, Holly little expects to meet up with Ben. Accompanying his grandad, he's wildly attractive, but annoyingly confident. However, after a bad start, Holly is drawn, irresistibly, to a more likeable side to Ben. But Grandad is grumpy, whilst Granny Jean is determinedly cheerful — and the entertainment hostess is more than a little interested in Ben. Holly is left wondering if this is good or bad!

JOURNEY TO PARADISE

Dawn Bridge

Lauren is on holiday in the Bahamas when a tropical storm breaks out. She is left in the care of Glenn, a very attractive American who takes shelter with her. They fall in love — but the problem is, he is the boyfriend of her best friend Anna. Lauren returns home racked with guilt, vowing to forget Glenn, but he has other ideas. Can they find a way of being together without hurting Anna?

THE RIGHT HUSBAND

Kay Gregory

All her life, while Kerry had attracted trouble, Declan was always around to rescue her — an unofficial guardian. She'd almost ended up marrying him. Almost, but not quite. At the eleventh hour her childhood sweetheart turned up to stake his claim to her. After all, Declan's marriage proposal had only been a favour to rescue her from a difficult situation. They weren't really in love . . . Yet jilting Declan at the altar was the hardest thing Kerry had ever done . . .

LOVE IN DISGUISE

Sandra Woolfenden

Everyone loves to read about singer Jasmine James, but often her publicity from the press is untrue. So when she goes away for just one week's holiday in Tunisia, dressed simply and wearing a wig, can she live like other girls her age? But, while she seems to be getting away with it, her falling in love brings complications she hadn't anticipated. Will David understand why she was forced to tell so many lies to cover her tracks?